DELIVER US FROM EVIL

FRANK FRANCIS

BLOODHOUND
— BOOKS —

Never let the truth spoil the dream.

PROLOGUE

It was the day Maureen Finn's life changed forever.

The White House was just as opulent as she had dreamed it would be. There was something so striking about the smooth, ivory tones of the walls, pillars and windowpanes that stretched across nearly every inch of the house, as if the entire building had been carved from chalk and bone. As she entered with the other guests, Maureen felt an undeniable sense of pride. She looked in awe at everything around her as the party were led by their guide, treading on either shining stone floors or vibrant red carpet as they were shown the luxury of the dining rooms, decked out in china and gold, while the woman sporting an immaculate blazer at the front pointed at whatever historic object they were closest to. They were afforded glimpses into the winter garden that she had seen in so many pictures, and while they weren't allowed inside, they stood outside the door to the Oval Office. Maureen felt distinctly affected by this, knowing she was so close to perhaps the most prominent and important room in the country.

Their tour ended at one of the large reception halls in the East Wing. As they were guided through the domed entrance, they were greeted by the flash of cameras and the murmurs of a smattering of press officers who had gathered around the giant room. There were military guards in their immaculate, gleaming uniforms stationed in various positions as the procession made its way into the space. One raised an arm tightly to his head to salute them as they passed. There were long tables with silk cloths bearing drinks and refreshments and a collection of pictures, showing presidents old and new and snapshots of various pivotal meetings over the years. Maureen looked up at John F. Kennedy, who flashed his trademark smile back at her.

Maureen was one of the youngest attendees. She had maintained a childlike brightness to her face, even though she had now passed thirty, her cheeks round and her saucer-shaped eyes with irises of a burnished, mahogany brown. The leverage granted by the heels of her shoes made her as tall as the majority of the men around her and she wore a smart but safe dress that didn't emphasise her slim figure, but didn't hide it either. She had kept her hair shorter in recent years, deciding this was the mark of an accomplished, professional woman, and she had carefully tucked the loose strands of her bob behind her ears.

As she continued through the room, she kept her head low and maintained a polite smile while avoiding eye contact with the reporters as she passed. It was as she made her way beyond a sprightly, glamorous blonde woman that her plan to remain undetected was undone.

"Maureen. Maureen Finn!" cried the woman, gesturing wildly to attract her attention.

Maureen sighed under her breath but projected her smile outwards and slowly made her way over to the reporter, who thrust a microphone a few inches in front of her. Maureen felt the large, square lens of the nearest camera swivel towards her in an intimidating manner.

The reporter began to speak, positioning herself adjacent to the camera, "We are here today at the White House, at a ceremony to commemorate the lives of Peace Corps officers who gave their lives in service. And I'm delighted to be joined by the award-winning journalist and author, Maureen Finn, whose father was among the honourees today."

She turned to address Maureen directly. "Maureen, tell us about the ceremony that just took place."

Maureen nodded and began to reel off a rehearsed response. "Yes, well it's a fantastic occasion of course and a true privilege to be here to celebrate the lives of the men and women who have given so much to protect the safety and freedom of this country."

"Can you tell us a little about the role of your father, Sean Finn?"

Maureen felt a pang of nervousness in her chest and tensed her muscles slightly to counteract it. "Well, I can't say too much because so much of his work is yet to be fully disclosed, but what I can tell you is that my father was a man who loved this country and gave his life to serve it."

She paused, suddenly feeling overwhelmed by the sentiment that enveloped her, and gulped back some of the dryness that had formed in the back of her throat before adding, "And on a personal level, it has been an honour to receive this recognition on his behalf today... he continues to inspire me and the rest of my family every single day."

Maureen smiled and turned on her heel to walk away, but the reporter had one final question.

"Is your father going to be the subject of your next book?"

"I haven't decided what I'm going to write the next one about actually. It's not a bad idea, I suppose!" said Maureen, chuckling graciously.

The reporter thanked her and Maureen headed for the drinks table. She politely chatted to the other honourees and continued to admire the beautiful interior that surrounded her, stopping at the portrait of the president she admired most, Franklin D. Roosevelt. She reflected once more on the gravity of the occasion and a surge of emotion shot through her body. Roosevelt, for his part, maintained his intense and aloof stare into the middle distance.

When she was finally granted a moment to herself, in the back of the car that drove her away from the White House, she took out the medal she had received an hour previously and held it carefully. The pristine gold caught the light and reflected it back. Her thoughts returned to her father, as they often did in her quieter moments. The medal was spectacular, but as she held it close to her, she couldn't help but feel that she would swap it in a heartbeat for more time with the man it honoured.

Hundreds of miles away, in a large apartment in New York, a man sat in a stylish velvet armchair, eyes fixed to the images on the television screen. The room was grand but bare, with next to no decoration on the bright cream walls and just two objects placed thoughtlessly on the marble mantelpiece. A framed letter, of sophisticated and careful penmanship and marked with unique stamps, and a picture of two smiling children, both no more than five years old. A little boy with his arms wrapped around the shoulders of an even smaller girl. There were large oak bookshelves pushed against each wall, filled with books, documents and photos. It resembled an office or the working room of an academic more than a place to live. A setting fitting of a man who had taken his work home with him and had never asked it to leave.

The TV was playing a live interview from inside the White House, with a perky, blonde reporter beaming into the camera. The man sat forwards in his chair as the reporter turned to interview another woman, who had a more delicate appearance. As Maureen Finn began to speak about the achievements of her deceased father, the man in New York chuckled to himself and shook his head from side to side. He had found his missing piece.

CHAPTER ONE

Maureen waited nervously in the wings, listening to the gentle murmur of hundreds of different conversations echoing around the lecture hall. Her hand twitched as she scanned the notes of her speech, her eyes barely taking in the words but the process itself making her more relaxed. Maureen was a confident public speaker, but this was another level. This was Harvard. The Kennedy School. She studied the smooth sheen of wood that covered the hall and took in the earthy fragrance that seemed to emanate from the walls. There was a noticeable hush in the noises coming from the audience and a voice echoed out:

"Ladies and Gentlemen, please welcome to the stage the renowned journalist and author, Maureen Finn, who will be delivering a lecture on her latest book, *Truth vs State: How the Watergate Investigation Changed America*."

Maureen took a deep breath and allowed the applause to run for a few seconds before she emerged into view. The lecture hall was beautiful, with rows of pews staggered back from the stage and two levels of boxes stretching out above them, all sporting that same polished wooden design. Maureen made it to the lectern in the middle of the stage, the width of the projector screen behind her. She placed her notes carefully in front of her, her heart thumping, and made sure to smile out into the crowd. There didn't seem to be a free seat in the entire hall, which pleased her. Trying to project her voice as well as she could, she began to deliver her lecture:

"Watergate was a pivotal moment in the history of our national consciousness. It was the moment that caused the average American citizen to lose faith in our respected and tenured institutions. To realise, perhaps for the first time, that the people who governed us were capable of dishonesty and deceit. The moment that we discovered that a president could lead a conspiracy to hide the truth from the public. Now, my question is this: was it worth it? Was the investigation and pursuit of the truth worth the political crisis it has created in its aftermath? Was it worth the uncharted, long-term effects on the relationship between America and its leaders? To put it simply: should we uncover the truth at all costs?

"Watergate marks a crucial collision of two opposing fundamental, almost philosophical, ideals: the belief that lies are unavoidable in national politics versus the belief that truth is a pillar of democracy. No news story in my experience ever dominated conversation, newspapers, radio and TV broadcasts the way Watergate did. Former *Washington Post* executive editor Ben Bradlee recalled: 'People literally couldn't wait for the radio and TV stations to read the next day's *Post* stories on the eleven o'clock news.' Nixon's downfall, spurred by the Watergate scandal, made legends of investigative journalists and rocketed the profession into the career of choice for young, aspiring reporters. As a journalist and investigator myself, I am proud to serve my country by relentlessly seeking the truth, uncovering the facts, no matter how important the financial, moral or even personal pressures. And I have benefitted from the increased desire of the public to question and challenge the decisions of those above them. As faith in our institutions has waned, journalists have become like goldsmiths. We assess whether what's in front of us is truly as good as it might look. And in my experience at least, it's pretty rare that our leaders present us with the equivalent of pure gold."

Maureen paused and allowed her words to sink into her audience. They responded with a collection of laughs and smiles and she felt a rush of confidence. She began to look less and less at her notes as the speech went on and allowed herself to enjoy the experience. The time seemed to disappear and before she knew it, she clicked onto her last slide, a picture of the same president who had been smiling down at her a month before.

"To conclude, I would like to quote President Kennedy, the man this wonderful school is named after: 'A nation that is afraid to let its people judge the truth and falsehood in an open market is a nation that is afraid of its people.'" She stopped and looked up and out into the expanse of the hall once more. "Thank you."

The audience rose as one to applaud. Maureen stepped away from the lectern and raised her hands in thanks. She couldn't resist feeling a sense of pride and accomplishment; the people clapping her were no doubt intelligent and cultured individuals and she had managed to earn their respect. There was a slight tingling sensation that vibrated in her arms and legs as the tension she had been feeling evaporated out of her body and into the expanse of the grand old hall.

An elderly man with untamed white hair and a suede waistcoat joined her on stage, joining in the applause. He was a professor at the school and had been Maureen's contact in the organisation of the event. He mouthed his thanks to her, which she accepted with a smile and nod of her own, and then he addressed the audience.

"Thank you, Maureen, for that wonderful and engaging insight into one of the core debates that shapes our social and political understanding. You are at the forefront of your profession, and it has been an honour to hear you speak. Maureen will be sticking around to sign copies of her book in the study room next door, so you are all welcome to join us for that. And now, one more time, a huge thank you from all of us at the Harvard Kennedy School... Miss Maureen Finn!"

Maureen was led through to another room, less grand than the lecture hall but still boasting walls filled with pictures and displays of the Kennedy School's achievements, past and present. Taking a seat behind a long table with a red silk tablecloth tucked neatly across it, she noticed that someone had taken the liberty of creating a decorative arrangement of her books, shaped into a semicircle. Maureen picked one up and absently flicked through it; the pleasure of holding something she had written herself in her hand had never really waned. The organisers of the event had held back the audience for a few minutes to allow her to get settled, or perhaps so that they could have time to come up with questions for Maureen or offer their own random anecdotes on the topic. It was nothing she hadn't experienced before and she enjoyed being indulged in such a way, by an institution as prestigious as Harvard no less.

The doors to the room were pushed open and the first members of the queue were admitted. Maureen placed the book down and smiled at her visitors. A small and sweet-looking lady of sixty or more was first up and she approached Maureen nervously, her hand shaking slightly on the spine of her copy.

"Excuse me, Miss Finn. Would you mind addressing this to my granddaughter. She wants to be a journalist, just like you, you see."

Maureen felt a wave of affection roll over her. "Of course; I am going to need to know her name..."

The lady aimed a tutting noise at herself and said, "Of course, I'm sorry. Her name is Maureen as well."

"Perfect," said Maureen, meeting her eye with a smile.

She wrote in the inside cover, carefully crafting the words with her pen:

To my namesake Maureen who one day will write a book that I will be happy to read.

She offered the page up to the lady, who lit up as she read it.

"Thank you so much!"

"It's my pleasure."

The next twenty or so people passed through in much the same manner. They might offer their favourite part of the book to Maureen or tell her a story about who it was for and why it was meaningful to them, and she made sure to react with genuine interest and engagement each time. It was a strange interaction, she thought to herself, as it was probably the only time she would meet these people and yet they had such a legitimate connection to her. It was one of the things Maureen most loved about writing; it was something that could be shared with anyone.

As she looked up from signing another copy, her eyes briefly flashed along the line to see the next recipients. And for the first time she recognised one of the members of the queue. An elderly man with thin wisps of hair neatly placed on his forehead and a face that seemed to have become permanently set in a welcoming grin. It was only his choice of clothing that had briefly confused her: a neat shirt and a well-worn, navy-blue jumper instead of his normal outfit of a cassock.

Father McCluskey was the priest of Maureen's local church in Boston and a lifelong friend of her family. He waited in line as patiently as the others and only approached Maureen when she turned in his direction. She rose from her chair for the first time and reached out her hands.

"Father! It's so kind of you to come."

McCluskey beamed back at her. "A member of my church has a lecture and book signing at Harvard University and I don't put in an appearance? What kind of priest would that make me?"

"I would have brought a copy to the church of course."

"Maureen, I have known you since you were a little girl. This is an incredibly proud moment in your life, and I wouldn't dream of missing it."

Maureen eased her protests and took the copy from his hands. Her mind clicked quickly; she had to choose her words to be even more poignant now. She took a little longer writing her message and then handed the book back, looking expectantly up at him as he read out what she had inscribed.

"To dear Father McCluskey, who has always guided and supported me through difficult times by giving me the faith to believe in charity, dedication and honesty."

The priest's voice crackled a little on the last words, which gave Maureen a strange sense of satisfaction.

"Thank you, Maureen. I don't know if I deserve all of that."

Maureen gripped his hand with the edges of her fingers. "I can assure you that you do."

The meeting with Father McCluskey left Maureen with a glow of sentiment that stayed with her for a while after he departed. She continued with her signing, not noticing the slight cramp that had developed in her writing hand or growing disheartened by the repetitive nature of the conversations. She reckoned that she must have been signing for well over an hour by the time the end of the queue finally came into sight. She allowed her mind to drift onto other subjects; menial thoughts like her route home or what she would have for dinner.

A man was up next. Maureen couldn't help noting that he was more handsome and neat-looking than the majority of her followers, despite her estimation that he was a good fifteen years her senior. He had an almost military edge to his appearance, the way he stood and dressed suggesting a methodical approach to life; the collar of an Oxford shirt visible beneath a crewneck, cotton-blend jumper. Maureen noted a series of small, linear creases beneath his thin, subtly greying hair, pushed and styled neatly to rest an inch above his forehead, as if even his ageing had been properly organised. It was his eyes that were the outlier. Maureen almost flinched as she met them; they were wild, intense and unblinking as they stared at her. For the first time she felt distinctly uncomfortable and quickly averted her gaze.

He approached the table and placed his book down in front of Maureen but didn't speak. She waited a few moments but eventually broke the silence herself.

"Hello, what's your name?"

The man continued to stare sternly at her. "Novak. Robert Novak."

"And do you want me to address it to you, Mr Novak?"

Novak had tensed his jaw visibly and was evidently deliberating over something, as his eyes flickered around in his head. He had his hand in his jacket pocket and Maureen could see that it was fidgeting within the fabric.

"Yes, thank you." He paused again before adding pointedly, "I just wanted to congratulate you on your investigative talents, Miss Finn."

Maureen, still unnerved by the man, muttered back, "Thank you."

Now Novak's face relaxed and he began to speak more fluently. "Do you know, I watched you on the television a month or so ago. You were speaking at a ceremony in Washington. You said some very interesting words about your father."

Maureen stopped writing and felt her blood run cold. She had always felt a mix of anxiety and excitement whenever anyone mentioned her father, but Novak's manner was adding a whole other layer of trepidation. Something told her that he was not speaking to her because of his interest in the Watergate scandal.

He continued. "It was funny to me, Miss Finn, that you spoke in such glowing terms about your father's accomplishments and yet it seems to me that you barely knew him at all."

The words provoked Maureen to react. "He died when I was

very young, but I have been raised on the stories of his achievements."

Novak laughed impertinently. "Achievements, you say? Well, I can assure you that whatever tales you have been told, they have missed out his greatest one of all."

He withdrew something from the jacket pocket. Maureen flinched instinctively and her eyes darted around the room in panic, but no one was close enough to be privy to their conversation. Novak placed a small, square and flat object on top of the page she had been writing on. It took a moment for Maureen to recognise that it was a photograph. She picked it up and held it so that she could see the image. There were two men in the foreground, the setting a dull suburban street corner. The way they were standing was odd, as if deliberately positioned a certain distance from each other, with neither looking at the other, or at the camera for that matter. Maureen felt her heart begin to thump hard against her chest as she recognised one of the men as her father, Sean Finn. Though she could remember little of him, the square jaw and strong bone structure were instantly familiar to her and, even though the picture was in black and white, Maureen knew that her father's eyes were a deep brown, like her own. The second man took her longer to pick out, as he seemed both familiar and yet somehow removed from her own life. He had a scruffy thinness to his appearance and dark, cold eyes. Maureen gulped to restrain a gasp when it finally clicked in her mind. It was a face she had only seen in other photographs, almost exclusively in history books. The face of Lee Harvey Oswald.

She felt her skin began to vibrate with anxiety and remained frozen for a second, her mouth suddenly devoid of moisture. She looked up again at Novak and stammered as she turned the photograph over in her hand. There was a scribbled date on the back, which read *November 1963*.

"What... what is this?" she pleaded desperately.

He remained stoic in his expression, though a smug smile was sneaking from his lips. "The truth about your father."

In one moment, Maureen's world came crashing down around her. The sensation was akin to leaving the flesh and bone of her body behind and becoming locked in a floating current of her thoughts. A series of images clicked in and out of focus: the picture of her father that hung on the wall of her apartment, staring proudly into the distance; snapshots of Oswald, including him being led away by police; another of him holding a rifle limply in his right hand. And finally, an image engrained into the minds of most Americans: an open-top, jet-black Lincoln Continental, with a handsome president inside.

Novak stayed looking at her for a moment, as if revelling in her confusion and anguish, before he leant in closer to her and spoke once more.

"I will contact you again. We have much more to discuss. But not here."

And with that he turned, replaced his hands in his jacket pockets and began to walk away from the table, leaving the signed copy, which he had clearly never had any interest in, on the table. The school had provided drinks and nibbles for those who wanted to stay after the signing and a collection of people had gathered in clusters around the room, sipping from glasses and holding pastries. Within a few seconds, Novak had almost entirely disappeared from Maureen's view as he strode purposely through the crowd.

It took a moment for her to wake from her shock-induced slumber. She looked once more at the photograph she was still holding: her father and the man who murdered John F. Kennedy standing together, during the month of the president's untimely death. Before she had a moment to properly consider what she was doing. Maureen found herself getting to her feet and yelling aimlessly after Novak: "Wait! Wait!"

Now the whole room was staring at her. But Novak had not

turned. As she became aware of the spectacle she had just caused she felt her cheeks burn with embarrassment. The next person in the line was a fresh-faced, spotty young man, who was now staring at her with a wide-eyed and confused expression. Maureen raised her hands in apology and attempted to create an excuse for her strange and frenzied outburst.

"I'm sorry, I thought he had left his book behind," she said uncertainly. "Looks like I was wrong." She hastily tucked the unclaimed copy under the table.

She slowly sunk back into her chair and after a further few seconds, when she felt everyone's eyes linger on her, they returned to their refreshments and conversations. The young man nervously approached her.

"Sorry, is it okay for you to sign mine now?"

Maureen's head was still spinning but she forced herself to concentrate and rediscover her polite smile, before looking up at him apologetically.

"Yes, of course. So sorry to have kept you waiting."

She slid the photograph out of view and tucked it into her bag, hung on the back of the chair. Returning to the young man, she went on auto-pilot mode, resuming her conversation and picking up her pen, but her focus was no longer on the event. Instead, she found herself speculating on her extraordinary encounter with Novak, asking herself continual questions and mulling over all potential answers. Who was he? What did he want with her? How did he get the photo? And was it legitimate? What did her father have to do with Lee Harvey Oswald? Was he involved in the assassination of Kennedy?

There was one question that lingered far longer than the rest; it was a question that had troubled her many times before. Novak's words echoed around her mind, like a backing track that she couldn't switch off.

Who was her father *really?*

CHAPTER TWO

When Maureen made it home that evening, she was suffering from a kind of emotional exhaustion that had only afflicted her on a handful of occasions throughout her life. Her body felt heavy and her limbs ached, but her mind was alert and sharp. She knew attempting to sleep would be a fruitless task. Instead, she allowed herself to sink into the sponge-like polyester of her couch and looked out at her apartment.

It had been her home for coming up to five years and was the first place she had lived by herself that truly felt like it was *hers*. The family home she had grown up in and where her mother still resided had been all she'd known for so long that the various dwellings she'd occupied afterwards, from college dorms to small and sticky studios above bodegas, had never quite matched its feeling of comfort and familiarity. Her current apartment had been selected after her first book was published and she had been afforded the luxury of greater finances and thus greater choice. So she'd put a lot of effort into making the place her own, filling it with pictures and books, plants and antiquities.

Her bookshelves were filled with everything from de Beauvoir to Carver to Michael Herr's *Dispatches*. Next to them, a shelf

laden with various awards she had received for her writing along
with her framed diplomas and a message scribbled onto a piece of
paper and signed by Kay Graham, the leader of *The Washington
Post*, who was one of Maureen's heroes. The A3 poster of Jon Bon
Jovi on one of her walls provided the first deviation from the
exclusively intellectual ambience. She wasn't sure if Kay Graham
would have approved of that. And dotted around were various
family heirlooms and memories: jewellery bestowed on her by her
mother and grandmother; a Celtics jersey that had been gifted to
her by an uncle. The only photo of her with her parents showed
the three of them walking on a beach that she couldn't recall; her
mother and father holding her hands as she wore a patterned
swimsuit and sandals. She couldn't have been more than four
years old.

And then, stationed centrally on the wall that looked over her
dining table, was the photo of her father. The one that had been
in her mind long before she had returned to where she could see
it. He was wearing his uniform, the cap tucked underneath one
arm. Maureen could recall so little of him in her own life that the
photograph had become a manifestation of everything her father
had been. She stared in silence at the photo, for the first time
looking upon it with uncertainty. Perhaps this had been the
problem. Her father was not just a photograph; he had been a real
person. And people were often far less perfect than their best
depictions might suggest.

Maureen left the couch and went to her shoulder bag, draped
over one of the chairs around the dining table, retrieving from it
the photo she had been given by Novak. There was her father
again, the same man who stood so proudly on her wall, talking
discreetly with one of the most infamous killers in American
political history. Maureen studied the image once more, scanning
it for any evidence that might call its authenticity into question.
She didn't want to admit it, but her experience as a journalist had
taught her that her first instincts were rarely proven wrong. If

something seemed off, it probably was. And if something seemed legitimate, you should treat it as such. As she held it between the tips of her fingers, there was nothing about the photograph that suggested it wasn't showing a real event precisely in the manner in which it had occurred.

The telephone rang, puncturing the solemn mood. It made Maureen jump, such was the intensity of her attention on the photograph, and she headed over to the compact card table where her white telephone was displayed and placed the handset to her ear. The voice that crackled down the line was instantly familiar to her, having heard it only a few hours before. It was Novak.

"Good evening, Miss Finn."

Maureen felt as if a cold wind had brushed over her, but she replied as calmly as she could. "What do you want from me?"

"I'm sorry for giving you a shock at your book signing, but I'm afraid I needed to get your attention. I can assure you that I mean you no harm."

Maureen felt a surge of courage and responded bitingly. "You didn't answer my question."

She heard a muted chuckle through the phone.

"I'm offering you an opportunity, Miss Finn. It is clear to me that you have a naturally inquisitive mind, a mind that always seeks the truth. And I have a lot of information that I think will be of great interest to you."

"I am not interested in besmirching my father's name. I can tell you that for certain."

"Please, let me at least tell you what I know and then it will be up to you to decide what to do with it."

Maureen stiffened. "Fine. Go ahead."

"I'd like to buy you a drink. Trust me when I say you will need it."

"Where?"

"Maurice's Steakhouse. Tuesday, 12 o'clock."

Maureen took her time to answer, chewing the edge of her lip as she mulled over the offer. She was deeply disturbed by Novak and could foresee a great deal of anguish if she allowed this intrusion into her life, but she couldn't repress her curiosity. This was something she knew she wouldn't be able to ignore.

"Fine, I'll be there. Now please leave me alone," she murmured coldly.

"As you wish," came the deep and measured voice once more.

<hr>

Maureen awoke on Tuesday morning with an undeniable sense of apprehension. She battled the nerves that were jangling in her chest as she got ready for the meeting with Novak. It was the kind of occasion she had no idea how to dress for and she subsequently changed her mind over her outfit a few times, eventually settling for simple grey trousers and a plain white blouse. As bland and neutral a choice as she could come up with. She took one last glance at herself in the large mirror positioned next to her front door and left her apartment.

Maurice's Steakhouse was located near the North End district of the city, a fair distance from Maureen's more central apartment, so she decided to catch a taxi rather than bother with the bus or subway as she felt like being left completely to her own thoughts. The taxi driver offered some desultory conversation when she first sat down inside but Maureen's limited responses brought it to a halt and she was allowed to stare out of the window in silence for the rest of the half-hour journey. She looked out at Boston, her city – her father's city – and felt the nervousness return.

It was only as she arrived at the restaurant, a very middle-of-the-road establishment with windows offering views of the bustling street and a selection of small, wooden booths and tables inside, all lit by dim, amber lamps, that she realised she was early. Maureen guessed from the layout of the place that it had previously been more of a classic diner, but the new owners had attempted to revamp it to attract a more sophisticated clientele. A smiley waiter welcomed her and offered to take her coat, which she accepted without thinking. She scanned the interior of the steakhouse, seeking out Novak, furious with herself for being early as it meant she would have to suffer the anticipation for longer. And then, as her eyes left the tables and found the bar, she saw a smartly dressed man on one of the stools, his body positioned to face the entrance. He didn't raise a hand or make any kind of gesture at all. Instead he just stared at her, his face fixed with a familiar stern expression. It turned out Novak was even more punctual than she was. Maureen took a deep breath and made her way over to join him.

Novak spoke first, gesturing to the empty stool beside him. "Hello."

"Hello," replied Maureen, taking a seat, hanging her shoulder bag on the back of the seat.

"Will you allow me to buy you a drink?"

Maureen stiffened and fixed him with a glare. "I'll buy my own, thank you."

The barman approached and instinctively looked at Novak, who grinned as he nodded towards Maureen.

"Hi, I'll have a glass of Chardonnay, please," said Maureen, and the barman disappeared for a minute or so, returning with a glass of light, golden wine.

Maureen took a tentative sip, aware of Novak's gaze as she did so, and then decided to proceed with the conversation.

"Before we start with anything else, I would like to know exactly who you are. I know your name, but that isn't going to be enough for us to continue discussing such a strange and serious subject."

Novak nodded and replied, "Very well. I run an investigation firm in New York. Specialising in looking into old cases. That's how I came into possession of the photo of your father."

"You're investigating my father?"

"Not your father." Novak paused, deliberately emphasising his next words. "The JFK assassination."

Maureen felt herself tense up. It wasn't a surprise to her, given what she had already seen, but hearing Novak confirm her father's link to the assassination was still damning. She was determined not to appear weak in front of him and snapped back as sternly as she could.

"My father had nothing to do with that."

Novak flashed a grin once more. "Are you sure about that, Miss Finn?"

Maureen felt patronised. She was growing sick of feeling that Novak had the upper hand, that he had information he was holding back, just to embarrass her.

"One photo doesn't prove anything. You're going to need a lot more than that."

"So you at least accept the legitimacy of the photo then?" said Novak, sitting back smugly.

"I don't think the fact that he met Lee Harvey Oswald is anything but circumstantial. A lot of people had connections to Oswald. The communists, the Mafia, even the FBI."

Novak let out a single dry chuckle. "I know. I worked for the FBI in 1963."

Maureen could feel her heart rate rising. Her mind was beginning to switch into investigative mode. That made a lot of sense. There was something about Novak that reeked of old-school intelligence agencies. The way he dressed. The way he held himself. The smug, smart-ass manner with which he spoke to her.

"If you've got FBI connections, it only increases my confusion as to why on earth you would be seeking me out with this information you claim to have."

"I don't have those connections anymore."

Maureen noticed that, for the first time, his demeanour had

briefly changed from its icy calmness. This delighted her and she pressed further.

"And yet you still have an investigative firm. It strikes me, Mr Novak, that if you are coming to me, of all people, for help despite all your expertise and experience, you might not be doing your job properly."

"As childish as your taunts may be, Miss Finn, you are not entirely wrong. I have sought you out because I believe that you can help me. In fact, I'd go so far as to say you may be the only one who can help me."

Maureen's eyes narrowed. "And why is that?"

"I'm sure it's fairly obvious. You have a rather personal connection to the case." He leant forwards on the stool, changing his tone. "To cut the crap, I'm essentially offering you the chance to save your father's reputation."

Neither of them spoke for a few seconds after that. Maureen looked Novak in the eye, something she had tried to avoid until that point. She felt on edge, a combination of adrenaline and Chardonnay heightening her senses. Novak had been testing her and she had challenged him back. She selected her next words carefully.

"So, all this is just some good old-fashioned blackmail?"

Novak sighed and ran his fingers over his forehead, showing a first glimpse of agitation. His voice rose and quickened.

"I appreciate that you may think a lot of your father. And that any indication that he may not have been the man you thought he was is going to be difficult for you, but I'm urging you to not let some kind of blind family loyalty overrule your logical, investigative mind. The truth will come out one way or another; surely you'd rather be part of finding it than left to deal with the consequences?"

The jab at her relationship with her father was one Maureen couldn't dodge. She found herself replying before she had considered what she was going to say.

"How dare you! You don't even know me! Who are you to come into my life and comment on my family? All you are is another conspiracy theorist, thinking they're the one to uncover the truth behind the JFK assassination. And I'm sure you'll put it all together in a book that a few lonely people will read, before it's discarded at the back of a bookshelf, picking up dust for the rest of eternity. Kennedy was killed by a lone communist fanatic. That's it. And my father, who was a proud and loyal servant of this country, had absolutely nothing to do with it!"

She found she was standing. Novak stared up at her with a look of surprise and disappointment. Maureen felt she had gone too far in her rant to return, and she raised her hand to get the barman's attention, asking for the cheque.

Novak attempted to rise from his seat. "Let me get this."

Maureen batted him away. "No! I told you I'll pay for myself."

He slumped back down and Maureen turned away from him sharply, leaning further over the bar. The barman produced the cheque and she paid it as quickly as she could. She returned her purse to the bag that hung on the back of the stool and cast a final look at Novak.

"Good luck with your investigation, Mr Novak. I hope you will respect the fact that I never wish to see or hear from you again."

He stayed silent, his clay-like face remaining blank as she left his side. Maureen collected her coat and left the restaurant, though she could still feel his eyes on her as she pushed open the door.

Maureen needed the taxi journey home to fully regain her composure. Sitting in the back of the cab, she noticed her hands were still shaking with tension. The energy and adrenaline were coursing around her body and she took a few deliberate deep breaths. Once she had managed to calm down and was able to think more quickly, she felt a few smatterings of regret that she had let her temper get the better of her. There was no remorse over how she had treated Novak, for whom she still felt nothing but contempt, but she began to worry whether she had in fact made the situation worse.

It was as they were nearing her apartment that she zipped open her shoulder bag to retrieve a pack of tissues and a compact mirror, feeling flushed and dishevelled. They weren't the first things she saw, however. Her heart sank as she realised the item sticking out of her bag was not one she recognised as her own.

A cassette tape, the classic rectangular, black shape, with a rubber band wrapped around it to attach another small rectangle, a smart and simple business card with the words *Robert Novak: Private Investigator*. There was a phone number at the bottom and in the space above the printed details a scrawled message in blue ink: *Call me when you've listened to this.*

Maureen peeled off the rubber band so she could study the tape more closely. There was another handwritten note on the front, though the faded ink suggested it had not been written recently. It was a date: *October 1963.*

Maureen held the tape in her hand, frozen momentarily. For a moment she felt a compulsion to roll down the taxi window and throw it out, discarding both it and Novak from her life forever. She resisted the urge. Once more, anger took hold of her. Novak had been one step ahead yet again. Maureen thought back to their meeting. He must have slipped it into her bag when she was paying the bill, with the dexterity and speed of someone who had surely done something similar many times before. Replaying the events, Maureen began to wonder if this was the reason he had attempted to pick up the bill at the end of their interaction, knowing her refusal would give him an opening.

When she returned to her apartment, she emptied the tape and card onto her table, along with a few of the other contents of her bag. It was as if the objects had a presence, as if they were watching her as she moved around the room. She retreated to the kitchen and opened a bottle of wine from the fridge, pouring herself a glass before impulsively drying some cups and glasses she had left on the rack that morning. It was an attempt to distract her mind from speculating about the contents of the recording. After nearly half an hour of further dithering, Maureen sighed and went to fetch her tape player from a drawer by her desk.

She sat at the table, her wine glass within reach, and popped the tape into the machine. She watched the small circles begin to whirl and heard the soft click of the machinery coming to life. Plugging in a pair of headphones, she sat motionless as the recording began to play.

First, a man's voice was heard; a deep and empty sound that echoed in the back of her ears: "Yes."

"Oswald? It's me. Finn." A second voice, a warm and vibrant Boston accent. A voice she immediately recognised as her father's.

"I was waiting for your call yesterday," said the first voice.

"I couldn't make it."

"You'd better stick to the agreements we make, otherwise you can forget all about me and our little plan."

"I will."

"You have the details?"

"Yes. I will fly tonight. Let's meet at the normal location. Eight pm. And take extra care this time, there are people watching you."

"Okay." The cold crackle once more, before the voices stopped and a gentle, distant ringing replaced them.

Maureen was paralysed for a few moments. She sat in silence, letting the end of the recording fizzle out, staring emptily into the distance. Blinking repeatedly to break herself out of the trance that had come over her, she replayed the recording several times, listening intently to every single word and nuance of the conversation.

By the third or fourth listen she was able to conjure an image of her father speaking the words, his lips moving to match the speech. As if the tape recorder had somehow created a ghost of him, like an ethereal jack-in-a-box emerging from within. Maureen felt two vastly different, juxtaposed emotions, occurring simultaneously. On one hand, she was stunned by what she had heard; a great, dark stain on her father's legacy. On the other, she realised that it was the only recording she had of his voice, a voice she had not heard in over twenty years and one she struggled immensely to recall otherwise.

She reached for the glass of wine and brought it shakily to her lips, taking small gulps. Maureen had nearly lived her entire life without her father's presence but had never felt so completely detached from him. He suddenly seemed to be a completely different man, a stranger from a different time. All the events of her life that he had missed came back to her. What would he think of her career? Her interests? Her boyfriends? The way she chose to live her life? What would he have said to her at her graduation? Or on the publication of her first book? What advice or guidance would he have offered in those moments when she had needed him most?

She looked up at the photo that hung on her wall once again, but no longer felt a sense of pride or even a shred of connection. Her eyes drifted from the wall to the window and she saw the bustle of the street outside. That was real life. He was simply a figure, a legend, that she had sustained exclusively within her imagination. And it was time to face the reality instead.

Maureen finally lifted herself from the chair and headed over to the card table in the corner of her living room, picking up the white telephone and dialling the number of the person she knew she had to speak to. The phone rang a few times before a familiar voice answered.

"Hi, Mom. I need to speak to you. Are you around this evening?"

CHAPTER THREE

The street Maureen had grown up on was one of those places that seemed perennially frozen in time. The same formation of wonky-looking, asymmetrical houses, with the same specks of dull grey and dirty white sidings. The same narrow road, just big enough for a car to drive down, but not by much. Sloping slightly, with the surface a makeshift collection of filled-in potholes and dug-up and re-laid tarmac. Always attended to by its residents and not the city's services, causing endless complaints in the neighbourhood. The windows of the houses matched the narrowness of the road between them, bearing a slit-like resemblance to splinters in woodwork. The garbage cans were out on the pavement, placed on the corner of each drive, finally granting some kind of pattern to the scruffy, patched-together setting. As she walked closer to her childhood home, Maureen could hear the distant laughter of children, a noise that transported her back to her youth.

This was South Boston, or "Southie", as it was lovingly dubbed by its residents. It was an area marked by an endless series of churches and Irish bars, the two havens of choice for the largely Catholic, working-class community. Maureen thought very fondly upon her childhood here. She recalled running with the other neighbourhood kids to buy sweets from Sullivan's, a convenience store that still stood just round the corner from her mom's home. She recalled trips down to Dorchester Bay, past the boulevard and along the waterfront, watching the boats drift in the distance of the shoreline. And perhaps most clearly of all, the St Patrick's Day celebrations, when every home on every street would empty to watch the parades come down, decked out in green and gold. The sound of old folk music and the light aroma of beer in the air as she became enveloped in the crowds.

She approached her mother's house, tucked just out of view on the corner of the street. When she knocked on the faded wooden door there were a few seconds before it swung open and the familiar warm beam of her mother's face greeted her.

"Maureen! It's so nice to see you."

Maureen hugged her mother, resting her head in the fluffy texture of her cardigan as she wrapped her arms around her.

Her mother, Jean, had gradually shrunk over the past few years and had comfortably settled into the stage located somewhere between middle aged and grandmother; her hair tinged with silver but only if you studied it up close. Her face beginning to wrinkle around the cheekbones, but only to the extent that it added extra character to her features. She wore a modest grey dress underneath the cardigan and Maureen noticed the trademark gloss of her lipstick. As her perfume rose from her body and reached Maureen's nostrils, the strong floral smell gave Maureen a pang of comfort. A kind of aromatic embrace that lingered after the physical version had ended.

"How are you, Mom?"

"Oh I'm fine, sweetheart. Are you hungry? I've got an apple pie warming in the oven."

Maureen sighed affectionately. "You didn't have to do that."

"Of course I did, it's your favourite!"

The two of them walked through the hallway and into the

kitchen, Maureen pulling out a seat at the central table while her mother began retrieving and reorganising crockery in the cupboards mounted on the wall.

"So what's the matter? I wasn't expecting your call, is everything all right?" Jean asked, continuing her pottering.

"Oh, nothing's wrong, I just needed to speak to you."

Jean turned to face her and raised her eyebrows. "That doesn't sound like nothing. Is it boy trouble? How's Bill? Is that still going on?"

Maureen laughed and shook her head. Her mother's first thoughts were invariably about her love life.

"Oh no, that's been over a while now."

"So, someone else? Oh, Maureen, please tell me you're not involved with a married man again."

"No!" protested Maureen, her cheeks flushing slightly.

Jean came to join her at the table, placing two plates and spoons down as well as a heatproof mat.

"The pie just needs a couple of minutes," she said. "I know you're always putting your work first, sweetheart, and I love that about you. All I'm saying is that after a long and stressful day, it helps knowing you've got someone to come home to."

Maureen smiled, touched by her mother's misplaced concerns. After a few seconds, as her mother was arranging the plates and cutlery around the table, Maureen took the opportunity to change the subject and asked: "Did you help Dad when he used to come home stressed then?"

"Of course I did. And let me tell you, if you're anything like your father, you'll certainly need someone to give you that escape from work."

Maureen pressed further. "Did Dad talk about work? I can't really remember it."

Jean leant back on her chair, clearly relishing the opportunity to talk about her late husband. "Well, that's because he never wanted to burden you with it, you were just a little girl! But, of course, he would talk to me. I told him, quite early on in fact, just after we got married, that I didn't want to be one of those wives who knew nothing of their husband's business. I wanted to be able to help as much as I could."

Maureen nodded but privately doubted her mother's words. Could she possibly have known anything of his interactions with Oswald? Would he have told her something like that?

Jean turned the focus back to her daughter. "So, tell me about work. Have you decided what your next investigation is going to be?"

Maureen's brain clicked into gear quickly, trying to invent a segue to begin asking the questions she wanted answered.

"I've had a couple of ideas. Maybe something to do with JFK actually."

"Oh really?" replied Jean, with evident surprise. "I would've thought there was already so much written about him."

"Of course, but you can always find a new angle."

"New angles! It seems we find a new angle to this tragedy every year!" said Jean bitingly.

Ignoring the outburst, Maureen continued. "I was thinking of my own perspective. American Irish from Boston. And my family of course. Didn't Daddy grow up with him?"

"Yes, they were friends in their childhood. Their families knew each other quite well, I think. And, of course, your dad crossed paths with him a few times when he was working for the State Department. I guess they sort of lost touch after that. He always spoke very highly of President Kennedy though. He was delighted when he became president. The whole street celebrated together."

"What did Dad do after he left the State Department?"

Jean paused, looking suddenly tired. She stared out of the window with sudden interest, as if she was expecting something to happen in the street. It remained empty. After an uncomfortable silence, she turned to her daughter.

"Why are you asking me these questions now, Maureen? Why the sudden interest?"

Maureen had prepared for this. "I think it's just that after receiving the medal at the White House on Dad's behalf, it has made me want to know more about him. To feel closer to him somehow."

Jean broke her curious expression and nodded solemnly. "I can understand that, sweetheart. Well, your father left the State Department in 1961 – no, it must have been 1960, we weren't married at that point. And he went to work with Uncle Marc at his law firm. He was a partner there."

"It seems a bit of a major career change to make. Do you know why he decided to leave the State Department?"

"He felt his work didn't matter anymore... and he wanted to focus more on family instead."

Jean had stuttered slightly through the answer, clearly changing the direction of the sentence halfway through. Her eyes left Maureen and darted around the kitchen. It was the first time Maureen could tell that her mother was lying.

"And was he still working with Uncle Marc in 1963?"

Jean's eyes narrowed instantly. "Why 1963? That's a strange question, sweetheart."

Maureen didn't flinch and replied swiftly, "I'm just trying to put the dates together in my head, to get a picture of my childhood, I guess."

Jean didn't respond and instead got off her chair, bending down to open the oven door and remove a beautifully golden and gently bubbling apple pie which she carefully placed on the mat in the centre of the table.

"That looks amazing, Mom." Maureen scanned the top of the pie and breathed in its rustic, fruity smell.

"I've got some ice cream in the freezer if you want to have it with that."

"Oh no, this is perfect. You don't need to do anything else."

The two of them sat in silence for a minute or so, under the pretence they were waiting for the pie to cool before they cut into it, though they were both privately contemplating how best to proceed with the conversation. Jean got up again and sliced the pie expertly, lifting a piece onto a plate and sliding it towards Maureen, before cutting a smaller portion for herself. Maureen picked at the edges, allowing the sweet, woody taste of the apples to glaze the back of her mouth before she swallowed. She looked aimlessly around at the décor of the kitchen, unchanged since her childhood. The various vases and antiques resting in the same places on windowsills and shelves, as if they had slowly welded themselves to them over time. A photo of her parents' wedding day hung on the wall opposite, which prompted her to resume her questioning.

"Did Dad have to travel a lot for the law firm?"

"Not really. Much less than he did with the State Department," said Jean, mumbling in between mouthfuls.

"So he wasn't taking impromptu flights across the country?"

Jean was sterner in her reply this time. "No."

Maureen chewed another mouthful of pie and deliberated over her next question.

"Did he ever go to Dallas?" she asked, immediately fixing her eyes to catch her mother's reaction.

Jean put her spoon down angrily and raised her voice for the first time in the conversation. "Maureen! What is it with these questions? I understand you were deprived of your father for a massive part of your life and that you want to feel closer to him, but this is not the way to do that! It's like I'm being interviewed for one of your books; like you're investigating me!"

When her mother did lose her temper, it was always with a mixture of anger and upset; her voice starting out firm and stern and then breaking on certain words as if she was about to burst into tears. Maureen felt guilty that she had provoked her, but the reaction had revealed a lot. One of the doubts she had upon arriving at the house had been dispelled: not only was her father's employment history now in serious question, but her mother definitely knew all about it.

Maureen backed down, having got some of the answers she was after. "I'm sorry, Mom. I'll stop." She tried to restore the conversation to a more casual and pleasant state, telling Jean about various pieces of furniture she had bought for her apartment and about her lecture at Harvard. Jean was clearly delighted at the news that Father McCluskey had visited her at the book signing and vowed to thank him next time she saw him. Maureen allowed her mother to cut her another slice of pie and to make a pot of coffee. As the night began to come in, she even returned the favour on the topic of her love life.

"What about you then, Mom? Any gentleman suitors at the moment?"

Jean scoffed. "Oh, Maureen, I'm far too old for that now. I'll leave the dating life to you and the other young people."

Maureen smiled, but a memory had appeared in her mind's eye. It was a few years previous; she had been out for the day in Southie, wandering the district's busier streets. It was as she had walked past a coffee shop with a large, emerald-tinted front window that a sight within had caught her eye. Sat at a corner table, with chairs facing each other, were her mother and a man she had never seen before. They were both looking away from the window and so never saw her as she stopped and watched them from outside. The image that had remained fixed in Maureen's consciousness for long after the event was that the man, who appeared older than her mother but still had a strong jawline and a warm, soft face, had taken Jean's hands in his and was squeezing them affectionately. Maureen had walked away from the window and had never confronted her mother about it, deciding that it was none of her business. It seemed her father wasn't the only one of her parents who had their secrets.

Eventually, Maureen decided it was time to return home and

leave her mother in peace. She helped her wash up the plates they'd used, despite Jean's protestations, and then picked up her coat and headed for the front door. Jean walked with her and opened it for her, and they embraced once more in the doorframe.

"I love you, Mom."

"I love you too, sweetheart."

Maureen went to make her way down the path, but Jean spoke again.

"Maureen."

Maureen turned and faced her once more. "Yes, Mom?"

Jean's face was stern again, the same expression she had used when Maureen had misbehaved as a child. "I know you're always searching for answers, but I want to warn you that there are some questions that don't need to be asked. It doesn't do any good. It certainly didn't for your father."

Maureen tensed her face in response, grinding her teeth together. She recognised her mother's words for what they were. Not advice, but a warning. She absorbed the information for a second and then relaxed her muscles enough to fake a smile.

"Don't worry about me. I'll be fine."

As Maureen walked purposefully away from the house and towards the nearest subway station, she let her hand drop into her coat pocket to find the edge of a paper card. She left her fingers on it but waited until she was out of view of her old street before she removed it and held it in her hands. It was Novak's business card. The one he had slipped into her bag, along with the tapes. She recalled the message: *Call me when you've listened to this.* As she continued to tread onwards in the dark Boston evening, she finally made up her mind what she was going to do.

Jean returned to her kitchen table after she had seen Maureen off, sipping the remains of her coffee. She could feel her heart thumping and her hand was unsteady as it held the handle of the cup. There was a desperation within her, an eagerness to act immediately, but she forced herself to count slowly in her head. Jean wanted to make absolutely sure her daughter was gone first. As she went past one hundred, she put the cup back on the table and rose from the chair. Picking up the phone that lived on a small table in the hall, Jean dialled a number that she had only ever called on a handful of occasions, but one that she knew off by heart. She waited nervously as it started to ring, before she heard a familiar male voice mumble a weary greeting.

"This is Jean Finn. I'm sorry to call so late, but I think we may have a problem."

CHAPTER FOUR

Maureen phoned Novak as soon as she returned to her apartment. It was late, but she was certain he would answer. Sure enough, after a few seconds, she heard the deep voice once more. It sounded more croaky than before, which pleased Maureen. She enjoyed the feeling of Novak being the one caught out for a change.

"Novak. It's Maureen Finn."

"Ah. Good. I take it you've been thinking over my offer then."

"I have, and I accept... on one condition."

"Yes?"

"I'm the one who releases the story."

There was a beat of silence for the first time as Novak considered. Maureen couldn't refrain from anxiously drumming her fingers on the back of the chair as she waited.

Novak's voice returned, the tone changed. "Miss Finn. I have been investigating this case, in various forms, for the best part of thirty years. I have staked my professional reputation on it. You have no idea what I have lost in my pursuit of the truth."

Maureen cut him off, sensing where he was going. "And that is a greater price to pay than potentially dishonouring my family's legacy?"

"That's not my problem," came the icy murmur in response.

"That is my condition, Novak. Take it or leave it."

A silence emerged, so Maureen spoke again: "Well?"

One word followed. "Fine."

Maureen smiled to herself. "Good. Well it would appear we're officially in business then. And that means I'm going to need any other evidence you have. You can't hide anything from me now."

"I've shown you everything I have," said Novak, and Maureen sensed some embarrassment in his words.

"Fine. I'll do some investigating of my own. I'll call you when I have something."

Maureen went to put the phone down, but she heard Novak's voice calling her back from the handset.

"Miss Finn?"

"Yes?"

"Now that we are working together, I want to warn you of something. This case is of an extremely sensitive nature. There are people who will do anything to stop the truth coming out. Be careful. And trust no one."

Maureen listened carefully. For the very first time since she had first spoken to him, Novak had shown a human side. There was genuine care and concern in his voice.

"I understand. Speak soon."

The next day, Maureen travelled to the Dorchester neighbourhood of the city. As the taxi pulled up on a charming, green and quaint suburban street, she spotted the house she was looking for. A large, detached and well-kept building with a pale white design and a slanted, tiled roof. The front of the property was bordered by a classic porch, accessed by a short staircase that lifted a couple of feet off the freshly mown grass. Maureen paid her fare and headed for the front door.

After she rang the doorbell, it took a few moments before eventually she saw the shape of a figure approaching behind the glass. She made sure that she was ready to greet them with a smile, as she heard the lock click and the door opened.

"Good afternoon, Uncle Marc."

Marc Randall looked older than she remembered. His hair was greyer and his face looked worn and weary. He was wearing a tweed jacket and a pair of beige slacks, which gave him the appearance of a retired professor. It took him a second to recognise her.

"Maureen? Is that you? Good God!"

"I'm sorry to arrive out of the blue. Is it okay if I come in?"

"Of course! Come in, come in."

He stepped back and hurriedly ushered her inside. He pointed her to the living room, which occupied almost all of the right side of the home, filled with light from the large bay windows. Her uncle had done well for himself, and his house reflected this, with the furniture smart and stylish and the walls adorned with paintings, some depicting Boston in times past. Randall gestured her to an armchair and sat in an adjacent one.

"It's so lovely to see you, Maureen. It's been so long!"

"Twelve years, Uncle Marc."

"Please just call me Marc. Uncle only reminds me how old I am." He chuckled at himself and then asked, "How is your mother?"

"Very well, thanks."

"Good. The last time I saw her was at our Uncle James's funeral. That's the problem with getting older: the only time that you see family is at funerals!"

Maureen smiled charitably at him. Randall had always been a

well-spoken and pleasant man, but he was totally devoid of charm. There was a clumsiness to him, as if he was constantly second-guessing himself about what was best to say.

"And you, of course," he continued. "How are you? I see that you've published another book! Wonderful! Congratulations!"

"Thank you."

"I was going to go and buy it from the store this weekend actually."

"No need," said Maureen, reaching into her bag to bring out a copy of *Truth vs State*, standing up and extending her hand to give it to Randall, who received it with delight.

"Check the inside cover," said Maureen as she returned to the armchair.

Randall did so and read aloud. *"To my Uncle Marc. An old friend of my father. And a trusted keeper of his secrets. With affection, Maureen Finn."*

Maureen watched as Randall's face twitched with confusion on the words, but in his relentless need for politeness he elected against referencing it.

"Looks very interesting," he said, placing it carefully to one side.

"Thank you."

"Are you working on something new?"

Maureen looked him straight in the eye. "That depends."

Once more, Randall was unnerved. "On what?"

"Marc, if you don't mind, I'd like to talk to you about something," said Maureen, trying to act as aloof as possible.

Randall shifted in his chair. "Of course."

"You were close to my father. And I was always told that he was close to John F. Kennedy. I wondered if you knew anything about that."

Maureen saw Randall's face twitch in discomfort. He looked away from her and bowed his head slightly.

"I'm sorry, Maureen, but I'm not sure I'm the best person to answer that. I would imagine you know more than I do on the subject, in fact."

"I don't know anything," said Maureen, coldly.

"What about that great commemoration for your father, at the White House?"

"That was a ceremony, not an explanation."

"I'm sure you could ask your mother," suggested Randall.

"I don't want to upset her."

"That's good of you," Randall replied ironically. "Digging up the past can be very upsetting for people."

There was an uneasy silence in the room. Maureen continued to look at Randall, focusing on every word and motion he made. Abruptly, he rose from his chair and cleared his throat.

"Maureen, I really appreciate you visiting me and for the kind gift of your book. Unfortunately, I need to get ready for another engagement. Why don't we schedule in another time to talk, so we can catch up properly?"

Maureen remained unmoved. "I really don't need much of your time."

"I am already running behind, I'm afraid."

Maureen knew he was lying. The way he was dressed suggested that not only did he not have anywhere to go in the present moment, but that he rarely met with anyone at all. She rose from her chair and picked up her bag, but as she started to walk out, she spoke once more.

"What a shame. I'm afraid I too am very busy, so I'm not sure when we will find a time to speak again. I just hope that when we do, it's not too late."

Randall stuck out a hand to block her path and spoke in a hushed but deliberate manner.

"Surely you didn't come to my house after all these years to threaten me, Maureen?"

Maureen smiled kindly up at him. "Of course not. I came here to give you a chance to help."

"With what?"

"I am investigating the relationship between my father and Kennedy. And his role in the president's death."

Randall reacted with shock, but Maureen could see it was feigned. "I know nothing about that!"

Maureen moved her head closer to him now. "We both know that is not true. And one way or another, your name is going to be involved. You telling me the truth will ensure you stay on the right side of it."

Randall's carefully rehearsed manner had been shattered and his expression was now fixed with uncertainty.

Maureen continued. "I will never ask you again. And this will be the last time you have to speak of it, I promise."

Randall looked up, as though thinking about who was in earshot. He grimaced and finally replied, "Let's go to my study."

He led Maureen further into the house, along a narrow hallway that led to the kitchen. Before they reached that, he stopped and opened a side-door instead, ushering her into the study. It seemed to have an existence totally separate from the rest of the décor, the previously bright colour scheme replaced by deep oak panelling. There was a small, square window that looked out onto the lawn and shelves filled with Randall's various pride and joys: diplomas, sporting trophies and family photos. A light aroma of cigar smoke and whisky drifted into Maureen's nostrils as her uncle pointed to a chair, while seating himself behind the central desk.

Randall sat back in his chair, no longer attempting any kind of receptive or polite posture. He looked defeated, exhausted even, not just by Maureen but from life in general.

"So, where do we start?" he said wearily.

"The beginning. You knew my father when you were young. What was his relationship with Kennedy back then?"

Maureen took out her notebook and made notes as Randall answered her questions, occasionally raising her eyes to check his expression.

"Okay. Well you'll have to forgive my memory. But yes, they were childhood friends. Similar upbringings, I suppose. Irish families. Ambitious. They got on well."

"What about you? You were part of the gang?" asked Maureen.

"Not really. I wasn't as confident or charismatic as they were." Maureen saw returning feelings of childhood jealousy flash across his face. "But of course I knew your father from growing up in Southie. We always stayed in touch, even after he'd joined the Navy."

"And what about him and Kennedy?"

"They stayed close. Your father helped JFK at political functions in the area when he ran for the House and then the Senate in fifty-two. To cement the local Irish vote, I guess."

"He had influence?" asked Maureen.

"Locally, yes," said Randall. "People always liked Sean."

There was the first notable pause in the conversation as Maureen observed Randall, wondering whether it was with fondness or envy that he was thinking of her father.

"Okay, and what happened as you both got older?"

"Well naturally you start to lose touch. I barely spoke with him after he joined the State Department in fifty-three. Once a year maybe. At school reunions, that kind of thing. And then, out of nowhere, he called me. Asking for a job."

"When was this?" said Maureen, scribbling furiously.

"Nineteen sixty, I believe."

"During JFK's presidential campaign?"

"That's right."

Maureen kept her face neutral, though she knew this had to be a relevant detail. Every further link she discovered between her father and the former president simultaneously ignited her journalistic instincts and caused a pit to form at the bottom of her stomach.

"This was when he left the State Department, right?"

"That's correct."

"And did he say why he did that?"

"He never told me details, I think he just mentioned something about wanting to settle down."

"And you believed him?"

"I was happy he called," said Randall, letting out a mild chuckle. "One of our associates had just left the company and I obviously respected Sean and knew that I could rely on him."

"And? How did it go?"

"Very well. For the first three years, anyway. Your father did a very good job. Brought in new business and so on. Seemed happy at home with Jean."

"And did he ever mention Kennedy during this period?"

"No," said Randall, his expression changing as if a long-forgotten thought had just returned to his mind. Maureen noticed immediately and pressed him further.

"What is it?"

Randall spoke slowly, piecing the story together gradually. "There is one incident I can remember. We were having a small gathering at home to celebrate Kennedy's inauguration. You've got to think we still thought of him as one of us back then. We all bought into the 'dream'. And as we were watching the speech – I will never forget, it was that line 'Don't ask what your country can do for you, ask what you can do for your country' – there was suddenly the sound of a glass smashing from the back of the room."

Maureen found herself absorbed by Randall's retelling and he grew more animated, setting the scene with his gestures.

"We all turned around to find your father with his fingers covered in blood. The thing had shattered in his hand! Blood everywhere. So, obviously we all rushed to help him. He was very apologetic of course, but I could tell he wasn't himself. There was an anger to him that I hadn't really seen before."

"Towards you?"

"No. Towards the president."

Randall's eyes homed in on Maureen after he spoke. She stopped writing for a moment and met his gaze, understanding what he was suggesting. This was a further nail in the coffin of her father's reputation. Randall was not only confirming he had a relationship with Kennedy, but that it was far from a happy one.

"And there was nothing that happened to cause this? There must have been a reason."

"He never spoke of him after that."

Maureen was undeterred. "And nothing out of the ordinary happened in the entire three years? Come on, Marc. Think. Anything?"

Randall did as instructed, reclining and letting his eyes drift around the room. After a few moments, he leant forwards and spoke once more.

"There was one time. It was an accident, really. A fluke. One of the secretaries must have messed up and a message got left for me instead of Sean. It was somebody from an intelligence agency – I can't remember which one – asking for Sean to ring them back. They didn't leave many details, but they said it had something to do with the Hauptman Case."

"What's that?" asked Maureen immediately.

"I have no idea. And I didn't then either. It was so strange, in fact, that I dismissed it as a wrong number or a nonsense call. I didn't even mention it to Sean, I don't think."

Maureen wrote out "Hauptman Case" in capitals and underlined it. She had no idea if it was important, but it was the best lead she had so far.

"One final question, Marc," she said. "You said a while back that things went well with my dad working at the firm for the first three years. What happened after that?"

Randall's face dropped and his voice became lower and more serious.

"He became more absent. Often leaving for days at a time with no notice. Missing deadlines, things he wouldn't have dreamed of doing before. The anger I'd first noticed on the night of the inauguration became more commonplace. It was difficult for me, because I'd known him for so long, but I... had no choice."

"You fired him?" interjected Maureen.

"Yes," said Randall bluntly. "It was best for the business."

"And when did you notice that his work habits had changed? What was the year?"

"Nineteen sixty-three," muttered Randall sadly.

Maureen shut her notebook. She had some of the answers she had been searching for and her pity for Randall had increased throughout their talk. She knew he had told her everything that he could.

She thanked him and got up to leave the study, but paused as something caught her eye by the door. It was a picture of her father, sitting on a large, leather chair behind a desk similar to the one Randall still used. There was a woman perched on the corner of the desk, both of them smiling at the camera. Maureen felt Randall walk up behind her and the two of them stood silently looking at it for a while.

"That was taken the year he joined the firm," her uncle said softly.

"Who's the lady?"

"Evelyn Ford. His secretary. A very good one as well. Your father liked her very much. And of course, she *loved* him."

"What do you mean by that?" asked Maureen, perturbed by his tone.

"Oh, just that Sean used to joke that she was his second wife.

She used to help him pick what ties to wear for certain meetings. Like I said, a very good secretary."

Maureen stared at the photo for a couple more seconds, taking in the details of the woman's face. Then she turned and thanked Randall again, before leaving him alone with his achievements and memories once more.

CHAPTER FIVE

The following day, Maureen rose early and headed to the centre of Boston to visit the City Hall. It was a building she was very familiar with, having made plenty of visits for previous investigations, but she was still struck by its clumsy yet imperious design each time. With its giant flat roof and jagged protrusions, she felt it would have been more fitting as a military base. It also looked as if it had been dropped haphazardly upon the clay-like plaza, bearing no resemblance to any of the surrounding buildings. Walking up into its shadow, stretched ominously out in front, was a somewhat intimidating experience, perhaps designed to scare away those brave enough to chase up public records.

Maureen pressed on and marched straight into the reception area. The bespectacled man behind the front desk stopped her and asked what she was looking for.

"The Public Records Department. Which is on the third floor, I know. I'm looking for State Department files in particular. Yes, I know where to look. Thank you."

She continued straight to the elevator, not looking back at the bemused expression on the man's face. His mouth hanging open, still making the shape of a word he hadn't got a chance to speak.

When she reached the third floor, the elevator opened out to a sea of tables, small desks and cabinets. It was on two levels, with staircases curving upwards at either end of the platform above. The line of filing cabinets stretched back for around fifty feet before meeting the back wall. Maureen sighed. This was thirty years' worth of Boston-related administration in one room. And she needed to search through all of it.

After a few minutes following the chain of signs that helped to filter the various departments, she was able to locate the cabinet relating to the State Department. She opened it and started flicking through the drawers within, searching for the years between fifty-three and sixty. The years her father worked for the organisation.

Eventually, her fingers slowed as she got closer to the relevant files. She found one segment which listed registered employees who started in fifty-three and started to look through the names carefully. Flanagan. Filbert. But no Finn. She pursed her lips in confusion, but carefully retraced her actions, checking the ordering system and making sure she hadn't missed the name elsewhere. There was still no sign of it.

Maureen opted to check the years on either side, thinking it possible that her mother's and Randall's memories had lost their sharpness over time. Still no record of Finn. She stood back, reflecting on everything she knew. Making sure it was definitely the right cabinet, the right file and that she wasn't making a stupid mistake. Nothing was wrong. She was in exactly the right place, but according to the public records her father had never worked for the State Department.

Two thoughts crossed Maureen's mind at the same time and she debated which was the most likely. On one hand, there was the possibility her father had lied to everyone he knew about where he was really working in those years. On the other, there was the chance that his records had simply been lost, either in an accidental administrative error or because of something more deliberate and potentially more sinister.

In order to remove at least one of the options, Maureen changed tactic. Retreating from the State Department section of the records room, she decided instead to check for any record on her father that did exist. There was an entire corridor-sized section of the room for checking old family records and Maureen moved along the floor adjacent to the shelves, her eyes fixed on the names of each file she passed. It turned out there were a lot of Finns in Boston and she found herself cursing her common Irish heritage for a moment, but finally she found what she was looking for.

Sean Finn. Her father's dates of birth and death on the cover. She opened it up, feeling a strange sensation come over her. As she looked through the vital documents that had been clipped together – his birth certificate, his and her mother's marriage licence, a list of addresses in the census records – it felt as if she were holding fragments of her father in her hands. Just nowhere near enough to piece him together fully. Then Maureen came across the information she needed. A recording of her father's occupation in 1961. *Senior Associate, Randall Law Firm.*

So he wasn't a phantom after all. There were records on him and concrete proof of what she had been told about his working relationship with Marc Randall, but with one glaring chasm in the information available. Whatever her father had done before joining Randall's firm in nineteen sixty appeared to be quite literally off the record. And it was fairly clear that, whatever it was, it had nothing to do with the State Department.

Maureen returned the file to the shelf. She felt that she had managed to uncover some of the mystery without actually making any progress towards discovering the truth. A sense of hopelessness drifted over her; there appeared to be no new avenue to go down. She took a seat in the records hall and opened the notebook she had taken to Randall's house, flicking through the pages and manically scanning the words she had scribbled in incoherent combinations of lists and sentences, desperately searching for something, anything, that would reignite her investigation.

And then, halfway down her last page of notes, Maureen stopped scanning. She noticed two words, written all in capitals and underlined: *Hauptman Case*. Maureen thought back to her encounter with her uncle in his musky study. What had Randall said? That someone had mistakenly left a call for him, intended for her father. Someone from an intelligence agency.

It wasn't a lot to go on, Maureen had to admit, but she endeavoured to be logical and systematic about the information. Hauptman sounded like a name. Of German origin. And the mention of a "case" suggested that whatever it concerned was in some way noteworthy. There was a story there, at the very least. Maureen reflected in this manner for a few minutes, before assessing that she needed to find out as much as she could on who this Hauptman might be and how he was related to her father.

Her new destination was one of Maureen's favourites in her home city, the Boston Public Library. She decided to walk the twenty-five-minute route from City Hall, along the busy streets of the city's most populated and bustling area, weaving in and out of fellow pedestrians on the sidewalk. The library was situated opposite Old South Church, an ornate Gothic building of cold, grey stone, with jagged turrets and a pond-green dome that peeked out between two of its tallest towers. Since Maureen was a little girl, she had always thought it looked like a home for an evil count and that it would be more suited to sitting atop a weathered hill in a dark and eerie landscape than on the corner of one of Boston's most tourist-dominated plazas.

Maureen crossed the road from the church and came to the library itself. It was far more geometric than its Gothic neighbour, but still undeniably beautiful, marked by a sloping red tile roof, frayed with copper edges. The main structure was composed of a lighter, sand-like substance and divided into two levels on its exterior, with the first sporting only small, rectangular windows, while above it lay a series of arched stained-glass panels. The architect had opted for arches again for the entrance, three this time, which funnelled the library's many visitors through to two great bronze doors.

It was the inside that Maureen truly loved though. She was greeted by staircases of shining marble, banisters mounted with lion-head sculptures, walls filled with magnificent murals, and mosaics adorning the painted ceilings looking down upon her. Every floor, corridor and turning was decorated with artwork and tapestries from centuries past. It smelt of paper and ink and dust and it filled Maureen with a warm, nostalgic glow.

The glow persisted as she continued up the stairs, making her way to the famous Bates Reading Room. The marble remained, stretching upwards into a barrel-vaulted ceiling with the open concave of a dome at the room's end. The terrazzo floor was filled with oak tables, all illuminated by the light of individual lamps, positioned over the surfaces of the tables like emerging flower bulbs.

Maureen quietly moved around the fringes of the tables, alongside the bookshelves that lined the walls, making her way towards an enormous, antique shelving unit, made up of four conjoined cabinets, all holding chute-like drawers. This was the library's card catalogue. And this was where she would find anything there was to discover about the mysterious Hauptman.

Her search began by looking through the cards organised by topic, which she considered her best bet. Pulling out the relevant drawers, she laid her fingertips atop the laminated cards within and manoeuvred them around, sharply dismissing the irrelevant selections with a swipe of her index finger. Gradually, she began to see cards marked with "Hauptman" in various titles and references. There was a lot to do with the brilliant Nobel Prize-winning mathematician, but she doubted that her father had anything to do with revolutionary research into molecular structures. She learned that a slight twist on the spelling was the German word for "captain", which again seemed useless to her.

Maureen was just reaching the point of maximum frustration, where she began to question her chosen method of furthering her investigation, when at last a subheading stood out that seemed to have nothing to do with the previous subject matter:

The Hidden Red of the Labor Unions: The Rise and Fall of Dirk Hauptman

Now that was a name she was not familiar with. Her eyes narrowed on the card, homing in on the date: the book was published in 1965. Not too far removed from the period she was looking at. She checked the reference number in the top corner, scribbled it on the back of her hand and carefully closed the drawer, easing it back into the cabinet.

Next, Maureen traversed to the library's labyrinth-like main archives, sloping in and out of the long corridors created by the giant shelves of books, frequently turning her wrist over so she could read the back of her hand, reminding herself of the number she was looking for. Finally, she found it. A small, tattered book that had lost the shine of its cover over time and was now a murky burgundy colour. It hadn't been published by any of the big literary names and Maureen doubted that it had seen more than a limited initial print run. She wondered if she was in fact the first person ever to take it from its position on the shelf, permanently wedged between two larger accounts of union activity in the sixties.

Returning to the Bates Room, Maureen seated herself at an empty oak table and switched on the overhanging lamp. The topic of the book was loosely about the unions' connections to Communism during the cold war and their attempts to rid themselves of it, which didn't pique Maureen's interest instantly, though she did concede that there was a semblance of a link there, through her father's meetings with Oswald.

She became impatient and skipped ahead to the index, to find the chapters containing information on Hauptman specifically. Her mind focused once more and she moved her face closer to the pages to read the sections she had found:

Dirk Hauptman came to prominence within the Unions in the fifties, known for his charismatic manner and excellent campaigning skills. Born into a German immigrant family, Hauptman had to cope with lingering xenophobia...

Maureen skipped ahead. She wanted cold, hard facts and she began to skim through the passages, looking for dates.

August, 1959.

She stopped skimming and made herself reread the previous few sentences.

Hauptman was present at the Detroit conference in August 1959, where some of his idealistic differences with his fellow representatives came to a head.

A loud, drained sigh escaped from Maureen's mouth and fled into the expanse of the hall, and she noticed a couple of heads swivel in her direction. She was beginning to think she was wasting her own time. She sat back in the chair and averted her eyes from the book, bringing her hand to her face to rub her forehead and eyelids, feeling that a headache was imminent unless she took a break.

Once more, she mentally revisited the conversation with Randall, replaying his answers. He'd told her that her father had helped Kennedy with the earlier elections, that he had influence locally. Could that influence have come from his relationships with the unions? Maureen considered this. It was certainly feasible. She had never heard mention of that before, but she almost chuckled, accepting that, in light of recent events, her lack of knowledge of her father's ventures was not much of a guide any more.

Her attention fell back onto the pages of the book. The Detroit conference in nineteen fifty-nine. Had her father been there? Was this how he knew Hauptman? Maureen sighed once more. She hadn't found any answers yet, but she was certainly asking new questions. As her journalistic experience had taught her, this wasn't the worst scenario. Deciding on a new course of action, Maureen took a few more moments in the grand and atmospheric reading room of her favourite building in Boston, allowing herself a brief period of admiration of a setting she had held dear as a child, aware of the bitter irony that this was one of the few foundational memories that she could still believe in.

CHAPTER SIX

The new course of action involved researching the most prominent Labor Unions in Boston and then trying to arrange a meeting with one of their senior figures. Maureen's search led her to the Boston Trade Union (BTU), whose head office was in Beacon Hill, and to an appointment with Tripp Harkness, their current vice president.

Maureen arrived early. The offices were located on a quaint, upmarket street, in a row of terraced red-brick houses, a few down from a local grocery, with carts of fruit piled high on the sidewalk outside. She had noticed a woman in an expensive fur coat walking a pampered dog and numerous mothers pushing their children in expensive strollers. Maureen cynically mused that this seemed a world away from the union's working-class roots.

The offices were behind a glass-pane door, raised by a few steps just above the sidewalk. She had been buzzed inside and, after hanging her coat on the adjacent stand, walked through the short corridor to a bright, modern and immaculate reception area, with plush but garish sofas set around the corners on either side and a large desk in the centre of the room, with a further few feet of carpet behind that which was filled with shelves and stands, each containing copies upon copies of various administrative forms. There wasn't a loose sheet of paper, nor one in the wrong place, and the level of organisation impressed Maureen. She had long wished that she could structure her case notes in a similar manner, but after several failed attempts had accepted it was just not in her nature.

There were a couple of men waiting on the sofas, having taken seats as physically apart as possible. One was wearing a cheap polyester suit and spectacles and was sweating profusely from his forehead. The other was in a white T-shirt and denim dungarees covered in oil stains. He looked Maureen up and down as she arrived, curving his lips into a perverse expression as he did. She ignored him and continued to the desk.

The receptionist sat in a swivel chair and was scribbling something down on a scrap of paper as Maureen approached. Her face was heavily plastered with make-up and her hair was neatly kept in place by clips just above her ears. She was pretty, Maureen thought, but looked uneasy and shy. She guessed she was new to the role.

"How can I help?" said the receptionist.

"I have an appointment with Mr Harkness at half past. I'm a bit early so I don't mind waiting."

"Of course, I remember speaking to you on the phone... I'll let him know that you've arrived." The inflexion in her voice made it sound as if she was asking Maureen if that was the right thing to do.

"Thank you." Maureen smiled charitably at the girl as she rushed to her feet and disappeared through a door to her right, returning to her desk a few moments later.

Maureen went and took a seat on one of the gaudy neon sofas, choosing the sweating businessman over the lecherous labourer as a sitting companion. She placed her hands in her lap and tapped her foot impatiently, eager to resume the investigation.

Ten or so minutes passed and Maureen found herself frequently looking towards both the young receptionist and the closed door that she had entered. A phone rang and the receptionist answered, nodding to herself. Maureen sat forwards expectantly. After a moment the phone was returned to its base and the girl looked over to her.

"Miss? Mr Harkness is ready to see you now."

Maureen walked briskly past the desk and opened the door, seeing another straight in front of her with an inscription that read "Tripp Harkness, Vice President". She knocked politely and heard a deep, booming voice that called her inside.

Harkness got to his feet as she entered. He was a tall, imposing figure of a man, with thin, receding hair on a giant boulder of a head. His shoulders were broad, evidence of repeated manual work, but a pot belly had begun to protrude below his chest, the buttons of his shirt stretched by the skin within.

"Miss McCluskey, is it?" he said, extending a pipe-like arm for her to shake.

Maureen had given a fake name to hide the fact she would be asking questions about her own father.

"What a pleasure," said Harkness, in a manner that was slightly over-friendly.

"Thanks for agreeing to speak with me, Mr Harkness," replied Maureen as he ushered her to a chair.

"Of course, of course. I spend most of my days talking to sweaty workmen, so it's a welcome change to have someone... like you come to visit."

Ignoring his obvious objectification of her, Maureen outlined her intentions. "As I said to your secretary, I am researching union business in the fifties and sixties and I just wanted to check some accounts with you. You can't beat hearing it from the horse's mouth, as they say."

"You're right there. Well, fire away, doll." He sat back in the chair, putting his hands behind his head but never breaking eye contact with Maureen.

"I wanted to ask about the Boston unions' history with John F. Kennedy. I'm guessing he could always rely on their support?"

"Of course!" blurted Harkness. "Kennedy was Boston's favourite son. My father completely idolised him; he was actually in the room for the 'City on the Hill' speech. The unions here were always fully behind him."

"Your father was also a union member?" asked Maureen.

"He was. That's how we operate, doll: following in our fathers' and our grandfathers' footsteps. There are many proud legacies in our unions."

"I see. So you must have records on all the prominent members from many years past then?"

Harkness sat upright again and looked at Maureen patronisingly. "We do, but I don't need 'em. I promise you, every name that's worth any salt in the history of the BTU, I've got locked up right here," he said, tapping his forehead with his finger.

It was a strange thing to brag about and Maureen was beginning to resent Harkness, a typical male figure in a leadership position, all bravado and minimal intelligence. Nonetheless, if he could live up to his claims then he had the answers she was looking for, so she decided to bite her tongue and play up to his ego a little longer.

"That's perfect. You're just the person I need then," she said sweetly. "Mind if I run a few names by you?"

"Go right ahead."

"The first one is Sean Finn." Maureen watched Harkness closely as he registered the name. "This would have been in Kennedy's era, around the time he was elected."

Harkness looked upwards at the ceiling and pursed his lips, contemplating it for a few moments, before he began to shake his head. "Nope, not ringing any bells. Any reason you mention him in particular?"

Maureen tried to mask her disappointment. "Not really, just heard his name in certain circles."

"Well, sorry to disappoint you, doll, but he ain't a union man. That's for sure."

Feeling the familiar sense of frustration return to her, Maureen swiftly moved on. "Okay, what about Dirk Hauptman?"

This time, Harkness clearly recognised the name immediately. His face froze momentarily and he suddenly became awkward and uncomfortable, finally looking away from Maureen.

"Can I ask why that one as well?" he said.

"Like I said, they're just names that I've come across a few times. There's no hidden agenda here, Mr Harkness."

Fiddling with the armrest on his chair, Harkness eventually mustered a response. "Well, then yeah, I've heard of Dirk Hauptman. Though so would anyone working in any union across the whole country, I'd hasten to add."

"Oh really? Enlighten me," said Maureen girlishly.

"It's just become a bit of a ghost story, passed on over the years. He wasn't a Boston man, though. We don't have those kinds of characters in our city."

Maureen's curiosity was growing. Harkness had gone from relaxed and confident to evasive and embarrassed. It suggested that whatever Hauptman had done was something that the unions were keen to forget, even thirty years later.

"And what kind of character is that, Mr Harkness?"

Harkness refused to meet her eyes. "I don't want to get into it. You're better off reading the endless garbage they wrote about it, lord knows there's plenty of it."

Maureen silently noted this, accepting that Harkness wasn't going to give her anything more on the story.

"One final question then. Even though he wasn't a union man, does Sean Finn have any connection to Hauptman, that you know of?" she said, her questioning finally bordering on the desperate.

"Like I said, doll, I haven't got a clue who this Finn guy is. I think you're barking up the wrong tree with that one."

Maureen gritted her teeth and clenched her jaw. Once more, the trail had run cold. While there was clearly more research to be done on Hauptman, there seemed to be no obvious connection to her father. And that was the bit she was after.

"Okay. Thanks for your time," she said.

The oversized vice president got to his feet and hurried to open the door for her, following her back out into the corridor. Now that he had proved ultimately unhelpful in her investigation, Maureen was keen to get away from him as quickly as she could.

As they walked back across the reception area, Harkness shouted some final words to her.

"If you ever need any more info on union business, doll, you just call and ask for me. Tripp Harkness. And I'll be sure to sort you out."

Maureen managed a weak smile and nodded, before turning away and heading for the front door, knowing she'd never need to speak to the man again. As she put her hand on the doorknob, she heard his echoing bullhorn of a voice again, but this time directed at his secretary.

"Sandy, doll. Be a dear and make sure my suit is ready at the dry-cleaners for later today. I've got the benefit event tonight. Oh, and choose me a tie. You gals always have an eye for those sorts of things."

Maureen stopped dead in her tracks. It was as if an electric shock had just sparked at the back of her brain. The picture in Randall's office flashed into her mind. The woman perched on the edge of her father's desk. *Evelyn Ford*. His secretary. The one her uncle had said had been like his "second wife". Adrenaline flooded Maureen's system and she felt a simultaneous sensation of excitement and then exasperation at not coming to the realisation earlier. This woman would know her father's schedule and, by the sound of things, she knew him more intimately than Randall did. Evelyn Ford might finally have the information she craved.

Maureen turned and looked at the rosy-cheeked receptionist, a beaming smile on her face. The girl saw her and looked back in confusion, obviously not aware of the crucial part she had inadvertently played in the investigation. Finally turning the bronze doorknob and leaving the union offices behind, Maureen burst out into the air of the Beacon Hill street, with a sense of momentum that had deserted her since she had first been thwarted at City Hall. At last, she was back on track.

CHAPTER SEVEN

When she returned to her apartment, Maureen dumped her bag and coat on the couch and headed straight for her phone table. In a thin drawer was a black leather book where she recorded phone numbers and addresses. She hurriedly flicked through the pages to find Marc Randall's name. She dialled the number and waited patiently, with the phone to her ear, as it began to ring.

After a few moments, the familiar awkward, tentative tone answered the call. "Hello, Marc Randall speaking."

"Hi, Uncle Marc, it's Maureen again."

Silence followed and Maureen could feel the panic rush into her uncle's voice when he finally spoke. "Maureen, I promise you, I've already told you everything I know..."

She cut across him impatiently. "I know, I know. Don't worry. That's not why I'm calling. I want to talk about my father's secretary, the one in the picture in your study. Evelyn Ford?"

"Oh. Yes?"

"I need to speak to her. Do you happen to know where she lives?"

Randall began to mumble. "Goodness, it was such a long time ago. I'm not sure I have any idea."

"Think about it," interrupted Maureen harshly. "You must remember something."

"Let me see. I believe that she married a Mr John Persico shortly after she left the firm. I think I was invited to the reception."

"Okay, that's good, Marc. What about an address? Where did they settle down?"

"Yes, hang on. I shall go and see if I ever made a note of it."

Maureen heard him place the phone down. She found herself absently twiddling the cord between her fingers, aware her heart rate was raised to a fast, thumping beat. Shortly, there was the sound of motion on the other end of the line and a weary sigh from Randall signalled he had the phone to his ear once more.

"Yes, here we are. The last I knew, they had moved to a house in Somerville. I have the address here: 17 Honeydew Lane."

Maureen smiled to herself and gripped the cord tighter in excitement. "Thank you, Marc. I really appreciate it."

She was already beginning to put the phone down when she heard Randall halt her. "Maureen. I want you to know that I don't want to be involved in this matter any further."

"I understand."

There was an uncertain pause between them, both equally wanting to end the conversation without rudely dismissing a family member.

"Thanks again for the book," said Randall finally.

"You're welcome," replied Maureen, and the line went dead.

Feeling adrenaline still surging through her, Maureen got straight on the nearest bus route, riding it for the thirty-minute journey out to Somerville. She enquired about the address Marc had given her in the information centre and was directed to an unremarkable street in the suburbs. When she located the right house, a small and ageing bungalow with decaying cream paintwork, she approached the door with trepidation. Trying to remind herself that this was, at best, a shot in the dark.

She rang the bell and waited anxiously, knowing literally anyone could come to the door. When it swung open and a sweet-looking old woman came into view, she felt a burst of relief. The woman looked at her with suspicious, slanted eyes but Maureen could already see this was the same face as the person in the photo. She beamed back at her.

"Good morning. Are you Mrs Persico?"

"I am," said the lady uncertainly. "What can I do for you?"

"I'm sorry to bother you, ma'am. My name is Maureen Finn. I believe you used to work with my father, Sean."

Maureen watched closely as recognition suddenly rushed to Mrs Persico's face. Her eyes widened and her face unclenched.

"My goodness. What a lovely surprise! Come in, come in."

Mrs Persico switched her manner to that of an experienced hostess, a role that Maureen guessed she had played successfully throughout her life, and stood back to allow Maureen inside. "I'll make some tea."

Maureen took a seat on the couch as Mrs Persico disappeared into the adjoining kitchen, returning after a few moments with a plate of cookies and two cups of steaming hot tea.

"You know, now you say it, you look a lot like your father. Around the eyes," she said warmly.

"Thank you. I'm afraid that sometimes it feels like all I share with him is a distant likeness."

Mrs Persico looked at her with sympathy. "I was very sorry to hear of his passing. He always treated me very well."

"I wish I could have seen him in that environment. You knew him better than I ever did," added Maureen, deliberately playing up the sadness in her face.

"You poor dear," replied her host. "Though I'm afraid it's been a long time since I worked at the Randall Law Firm, and my memory is not what it once was."

"Surely there must be some stories you can tell me? I bet my Uncle Marc could be a difficult man to work with..."

Mrs Persico laughed and sighed, and Maureen sensed she was winning her over. "Oh, you're right about that. He was totally harmless, Marc, but he was painfully... dull. Me and the rest of the girls used to giggle at him behind his back."

Maureen sat forwards. "But you worked directly for my father, didn't you? As his secretary?"

"That's right," she replied warmly. "I was young, it was my first job really. I was very proud of it as I was the only one of my friends who had an actual office job!"

"And what was it like working with him?"

Mrs Persico smiled. "I loved working for Sean. He was very courteous, polite and kind. Demanding, of course. He expected you to keep up with him. But he would never shout, never curse. He was a proper gentleman, I suppose, the kind you don't seem to get any more."

Her words were genuine and heartfelt, and Maureen enjoyed the experience of remembering her father in such a positive light. She took a cookie from the plate and ate it slowly as she continued her questions.

"I know that my father left the firm in nineteen sixty-three. Do you know why that was?"

Mrs Persico's smile faded. The suspicion that had initially appeared on her face returned.

"I was just a secretary. I couldn't say I knew the full story. Why?"

"I'm just trying to piece together some details about him. As I said, it feels like I hardly knew him at all."

"That must have been hard, growing up without your father's presence," said Mrs Persico, pausing to consider her next words more carefully. "One day, your father had some visitors come to the office. That's when everything changed."

"Visitors?" asked Maureen.

"Yes. Unannounced. Suzy, one of the other girls that worked there, came to me and said that Mr Finn had some people waiting to see him. It was odd as I had nothing on the agenda for that day. She said that they had told her they used to work with your father, so I figured I should let them in. Well, he was just as surprised as I was."

"And you didn't know who they were?"

"No. They didn't seem like the business associates we normally got at the office. They were colder and quieter. Not trying to crack a joke or flirt with me or the other girls. Your father shut the office door so I never heard what they were discussing but after a while I could definitely hear shouting."

"And then what happened?"

"Well, it was the strangest thing. The door opened and your father followed the men outside. It was like he had been arrested! And all he said to me was that he had to leave and would be back tomorrow. No mention of where he was going or for me to cancel any plans." She stopped suddenly and stared absently out of the window, showing a worry that Maureen couldn't work out was for herself or for her father all those years before. "And I watched him get in the back of a car with them. He had such a strange look on his face. Like he was resigned to whatever they were asking of him."

Maureen was transfixed by her retelling. This had to be connected with the taped conversation with Oswald. It explained the behaviour that Randall had described in the latter stages of his work at the firm. She wanted more detail. A name. A message. Some kind of evidence.

"They must have mentioned something. A note of some kind?"

Mrs Persico flinched. Her eyes withdrew from Maureen and she sunk back in her chair.

"What is it?" asked Maureen, her tone heightened so that she was almost shouting.

"I don't want to talk about that. Please, Maureen, can we move on from this?"

Maureen sighed and tried to soften her voice. "Mrs Persico, you are my last hope. No one will tell me the truth about my father. I just want to understand what happened to him. Please."

She watched as a tear came to the older woman's eye. "My husband told me not to say anything. He doesn't want me to be involved."

Maureen came to a realisation. "I'm not the first person to ask you about this, am I?"

Mrs Persico shook her head solemnly. "They came back after your father left the firm. Secret service men. Asked me what I knew. If there had been a note left behind."

"What did you tell them?"

"Nothing!" said Mrs Persico, tearful anger spilling out of her. "I would never have said anything that could hurt your father. But... it affected me. I left the firm as soon as I could after that."

Maureen left the couch and came over to kneel in front of her. She took her hand in her palm and looked up at her watery eyes.

"I want to thank you for your loyalty to my father. You have been very brave and I'm sorry that you were involved in this," she said, as earnestly as she could. "All I'm asking is that you allow me to take the burden from you now. It sounds like you've been carrying it for far too long."

At that moment there was the noise of the front door clicking open. Mrs Persico hurriedly detached her hands from Maureen and leant away from her. There was a call from the doorway and a few seconds later a tall, weary-looking man entered the living room. Mr Persico. His eyes narrowed when he saw Maureen kneeling in front of his wife's chair. He had a face that looked as if it had permanently frozen in a snarl.

"What's going on here?"

Maureen found herself unsure of what to say and looked to Mrs Persico.

"Oh hello, dear. This young person is conducting a survey for the city," she said.

"Survey?" replied Mr Persico, glaring at Maureen.

"Yes. I just finished, in fact," said Maureen, getting back to her feet and going to retrieve her bag from the couch.

She felt both pairs of eyes on her as she made her exit. Her chance of getting anything from Mrs Persico was slipping away.

"I'll show you out," grumbled Mr Persico.

Maureen took one last chance to look at Mrs Persico, trying to do the talking with her expression. "Thank you for your time, ma'am. It will prove invaluable, I'm sure."

Mr Persico opened the door and Maureen stepped outside.

"Next time send a letter. I don't like people poking their nose in our business unannounced," he muttered and then slammed the door behind her.

Maureen stood motionless for a few seconds, dejected at the opportunity for new information being stolen from her. Eventually, she sighed deeply and turned, ready to start the journey back to Boston. The sound of the door clicking behind her made her look back over her shoulder.

Mrs Persico was tiptoeing out of the house, with a ruby-red folder in her hands. She caught up with Maureen and held it out to her.

"Excuse me, madam. You forgot your paperwork."

"My paperwork?"

Mrs Persico's eyes told the story. "Yes... you wouldn't want to have left this behind."

Maureen caught on and smiled warmly at her. "Thank you very much. And thank you for the tea."

Mrs Persico returned her smile and before she scampered back to the house said, "You really do look like your father."

Maureen clutched the folder tightly in her grasp until she was back on the bus. She made sure to sit near the back, with no one near her, and then she opened it to see what was inside. It was essentially a large diary, with wide columns for every day of the year ninety sixty-three. There were numerous messages on each page, in neat, sophisticated handwriting. This was the calendar Mrs Persico had kept for her father, with details of every meeting and appointment he had during the period. Maureen combed carefully through each page, until she reached the month of May, and a note fell out into her lap. Before she read it, she continued flicking through, noticing that from May onwards the pages got emptier and emptier. Her father had been a busy man at the start of the year and then, all of a sudden, he was free as a bird.

Maureen took the note that had fallen out and held it up to read. The handwriting was different and was therefore not written by Mrs Persico. This must have been what was left behind on the day the men visited her father.

> Dear Sean,
> I apologise for contacting you in such a discourteous manner. You will soon appreciate that the nature of the situation warrants such urgency and reticence. I am calling for you to attend a meeting where this matter will be better explained. Please go with my colleagues willingly, who will escort you to the location. As stated, my apologies at not being able to disclose more at this stage.
> Kind regards,
> Clipper.

Maureen breathed out and looked away to stare out of the window, allowing the information to process in her mind. A plan started to form as her brain ticked along frantically. She needed to speak to Novak as soon as possible. The investigation was finally starting to take shape.

CHAPTER EIGHT

Located in the Back Bay district of the city was the Charles River Esplanade, a picturesque stretch of state-owned parkland running alongside Boston's most famous waterway. A few feet from the start of the path was an Irish pub, McGettigan's, a grizzled establishment with outside seating under large green parasols, and bunting and shamrock wallpaper on the walls inside.

Maureen and Novak sat at one of the tables inside the main room, Maureen on a banquette tucked against the wall and Novak on a chair opposite her. They had ordered coffees but neither had taken much more than a sip. It was early in the day and the place wasn't busy so they could speak openly to each other. On the table lay Maureen's notebook, opened on the relevant pages of notes and the scrap of paper that she had found in Mrs Persico's folder.

"Clipper?" said Novak, sounding the word out to himself.

"Does it mean anything to you?"

"No," said Novak, still lost in thought.

"First name or last name?"

"I have no idea." He let his face drop into his palm, before muttering, "It could be a code name, I suppose."

"What makes you say that?"

Maureen raised her eyebrows and watched Novak. He had leant back in the chair with his legs stretched out in front of him at an angle, one arm resting on the back of the chair and the other hanging down, which he used as a tool to illustrate while he spoke.

"It's an intelligence agency thing. I've seen similar ones used hundreds of times before, but I don't recognise it."

"Okay, well is there anyone who might know?"

"I doubt it. Those names are as classified as it gets. I doubt there are more than ten people in the world who know Clipper's real identity."

"Well, apparently my father was one of them," said Maureen, furrowing her brow.

"What else have you found?" asked Novak, and Maureen wondered if he was deliberately changing tack.

"The other thing that Marc Randall told me about was a voice message that mentioned something he called the Hauptman Case. I went to look at the public records at City Hall and I couldn't find any record of my father ever working for the State Department."

Novak's eyes flickered downwards for a moment.

"What? You don't seem surprised by that."

Novak returned to looking at her and sighed. "I can imagine that you already have your suspicions. Look at what you've found so far. The voice message, the men coming to the office. The note. The fact that your father clearly knew who Clipper was and the fact that his word was enough to convince him to be blindly escorted away."

Maureen already knew where he was going. "My father... worked in intelligence?"

Novak didn't speak but nodded solemnly, like a grumpy

teacher accepting a tired answer from his class.

Maureen's voice quickened. "He didn't work with you in the FBI?"

Novak shook his head. "Not the FBI. The CIA."

Maureen slumped back on the banquette. Novak had been right; she'd had her suspicions, but nothing to prepare her for the bombshell that her father had worked for the world's biggest intelligence agency. Once more, the picture of him she held in her mind, a replica of the one that hung in her apartment, became distorted. Her shock and confusion subsided, replaced by a burning anger.

"You knew this and didn't tell me."

Novak flinched and attempted to respond but Maureen cut him off.

"I told you that you weren't to hide anything from me now! What are you doing? I'm trying to investigate and you're still playing your stupid games!"

"Maureen. It isn't like that..."

Maureen found herself rising from the table and snatching the notes firmly in her grasp. She knew that some of the anger she was feeling wasn't directed at Novak but at her father and his secrets, but she only had one person she could take it out on. Her skin was hot and her limbs trembled.

"I gave you a chance. I'm going to do this on my own. I don't need you and your lies."

She stormed out of the pub, marching past the benches and green parasols, her rage carrying her forwards at a pace close to a jog. After a few moments, there was the sound of gravel crunching underfoot behind her and Novak, breathing heavily, frantically trying to catch up with her.

"Are you not going to let me explain?" he asked, almost yelling at her, his words rasping and exaggerated.

"I am sick and tired of people lying to me. Leave me alone!"

"Do you always run away when someone upsets you?" he said, with a tone of malice.

Maureen turned towards him and her body seemed to lock up. She was ready to punch him, scratch at him or whatever else she could do to wipe that smug expression off his face. Just about stopping herself, she gritted her teeth and spat back: "You're the one who got me involved in this, let's be very clear about that. And in barely a week I've found out more about this case than you managed in thirty years. And you're going to stand there and take the moral high ground? Screw you."

As she went to leave, Novak stuck out an arm and clasped her wrist. His grip was so firm that it stopped her dead in her tracks. She tried to battle free but he looked up at her, his face calm and his eyes as soft as she had ever seen them. It was almost hypnotic and she soon found herself standing still and ceasing to struggle.

"I'm sorry. You're right. If this is work, we need to be completely honest with each other," he said, still fixing her with the intense stare. "Let's take a walk."

They abandoned their coffees and headed for the esplanade. It was a beautiful part of the city. The sun shone down and caught the surface of the river, making it gleam, while the trees that lined either side of the pathway were covered with delicate, pink blossom that fell to create thin petalled carpets on the grass below. The path was lined with people, ranging from joggers to couples strolling hand in hand. Maureen and Novak walked slowly and the pleasant breeze helped to cool her temper.

They walked in silence for the first few metres of the path, until Novak spoke, starting a completely new topic of conversation.

"I really am sorry that you grew up without a father," he said, in a heartfelt manner.

Maureen was taken aback by this show of kindness and took a few seconds to mutter her thanks.

"I think of my own father," Novak continued. "He was born in

Czechoslovakia and came to this country to raise a family. Super hardworking. I guess that's why I'm the way I am really. He used to take me hunting when I was young. And he'd say, 'Don't give up, Robert. The right moment will always come. Make sure you're ready for it.'"

Maureen found herself affected by the story. "Is that what you've been doing with this case? Waiting for the right moment?"

Novak chuckled. "I guess so. And seeing you at the White House, I knew that moment had arrived."

"Then don't mess it up," said Maureen, expressionlessly.

They crossed over a small bridge with black iron railings to get from one side of the river to the other. Maureen looked down at the ducks swimming below, following tightly behind each other like cars in a line of traffic. Eventually, they came to a series of benches that overlooked a wider stretch. They picked one of the benches at random and sat down, looking out at the scenery.

"So, how do you know about my father working for the CIA?" asked Maureen.

Novak sighed and then began his explanation. "I first met your father in fifty-nine. He interviewed me."

"I thought you worked for the FBI?" Maureen interjected.

"I didn't say I passed the interview," replied Novak, with a grimace.

"I see. So is that why you hate my father?"

Novak bristled and looked away from her. "I never said I hated your father, Maureen. Quite the contrary, in fact. I admired him hugely. He was a very impressive man in those days. A big reputation within the intelligence world. I think that might have been the problem in my interview. I was intimidated by him."

Maureen stayed quiet, aware that Novak was finally being open and honest with her. Hearing his inferiority complex compared to her father shed light on a different side of his personality. He appeared vulnerable and insecure for the first time.

"Anyway, I joined the FBI a few months later. And it wasn't long after that when the news spread that your father had left the CIA. It was quite the story back then. Like I said, he had quite a reputation. There were all kinds of rumours flying around: that he'd been asked to quietly step away; that he was too close to a Soviet agent; that there was some kind of scandal."

"And you believed the rumours?" asked Maureen.

"Not in the slightest. I just got on with my job, which was taking care of a few troublemakers. No one major at that stage. Small players, communists, Castro supporters. One of the people I kept tabs on was an ex-marine returning to the US from the Soviet Union in sixty-two."

"Oswald," said Maureen knowingly.

"That's right."

"So that's how you got the photo and the tape of my father speaking to him." Maureen was starting to get a clearer picture of everything.

"I couldn't believe my eyes, of course. I thought, how could a man like Sean Finn be involved with someone like Oswald?"

"How many times did they meet?"

"Three times at least. In the weeks and days directly before the assassination."

"And what did you do about it?"

Novak paused and chewed on his lip for a few moments. "I reported it straight away. Up the chain of command. Got the normal nonsense back. 'Good job.' 'Sit tight.' All that rubbish. And then I was called into head office. A guy called Liam McCarthy. A proper hotshot. He called me into his office, offered me a glass of bourbon. He was very complimentary about me at first, but I quickly worked out where it was going. He told me to forget about the case. To leave it to the big boys."

"And I'm guessing nothing ever came of it?"

"Never heard mention of it again," said Novak sadly.

"They covered it up? That's disgraceful. This changes

everything we know about the assassination. You should have given evidence at the Warren Commission. My father should have been a key witness!" Maureen shouted, the injustice boiling up inside her.

"I know," said Novak. "And after a while, I couldn't stand it. Watching everything that happened after. Jack Ruby. That sham of a Commission. All the hysteria about the bullet. I lost faith in the Bureau; I quit to start my own investigation firm in New York, but they made me sign a waiver when I left, basically guaranteeing my silence. That's why I've had to investigate so quietly since. They could put me in federal prison if they find that I've been spilling secrets."

"The picture and the tapes? How did you..." started Maureen.

"I made copies. Smuggled them out. It was a huge risk but without them I had nothing."

There was a moment of silence. Maureen nodded slowly, finally appreciating the strain that Novak had been under and what he had already staked on the investigation. She had a new sense of admiration for him. He clearly shared her investigative determination to get to the truth, whatever the cost.

"So you need me because I can investigate without arousing suspicion," she said.

"Exactly," said Novak. "You can ask the questions I have wanted to, under the guise of writing a new book. It was just a bonus that you had certain personal connections as well."

Maureen breathed out emphatically. "So... what now?"

"I will look further into the Hauptman Case. That can't be related to Oswald so it won't be as difficult to get information on. The unions may be unwilling to talk about it themselves, but I've got an old friend who might help me out."

"And what about me?"

Novak fell quiet for a moment and looked out towards the water that stretched out in front of them. It was clear that he knew exactly what he was going to ask of her, but felt uncomfortable about it.

"I have an idea. There's a former contact at the Bureau. He took over all of my cases when I left; he'll have seen the records I made on your father."

"You want me to talk to him?" asked Maureen, still in the dark.

"Yeah. You'll need to go to Washington."

"I'm happy to do that."

Novak still looked guilty, his eyes having now fallen to fix on his shoelaces.

"What is it?" asked Maureen impatiently.

"His name is Don Cassidy," said Novak. "And he... has a bit of a reputation."

"What kind of reputation?" asked Maureen anxiously.

Novak finally looked at her again, his eyebrows raised. "Let's just say he has a certain weakness for women."

Maureen began to understand. Novak's shifty and uneasy manner was borne not out of fear but from a bumbling nervousness to address her sexuality. It came as a relief to her. There were many things she would have found herself ill-equipped to deal with within the investigation, but sleazy womanisers was not one of them.

"Right," she said, resisting the urge to giggle. "So you think he'll be happy to talk to me specifically then?"

Novak's eyes flashed with panic as he found himself unsure how to respond. "Believe me, I wouldn't ask you if I didn't think it was important."

"It's fine, honestly," said Maureen, secretly enjoying his discomfort.

"Just be careful," he said, lowering his tone deliberately.

"I can look after myself," she snapped back.

"You don't know Cassidy. It might seem like you're there to

discuss your father, but that won't be what he hopes to get out of the meeting."

Maureen raised her nose in mild disgust and looked away, hoping to move on to a different topic. As she did so, her attention was caught by the inscription on the back of the bench, engraved on a grey plaque in its centre.

In Memory of Oliver Harrington. Beloved Husband, Father and Grandfather
March 4th 1901 – November 11th 1989

She read aloud, alerting Novak to its existence.

"Quite a life," he observed. "Nearly the whole twentieth century. He would have seen it all."

"It's funny, isn't it. You're right, he probably had a remarkable life, full of stories and experiences. And then once you're gone, you're remembered as a husband, father and grandfather. Nothing else."

"That's not so bad, surely," said Novak, looking out wistfully over the water. "I'd certainly take that."

Maureen noticed his change in mood. "Have you got children of your own?"

"A boy and a girl," he replied. "They're with their mother."

"Divorced?"

"We've been separated for a while."

Maureen watched him closely. His face dropped and he recoiled as if feeling a pain shoot through his body. She decided not to press him further. They stayed on the bench for a while, finally speaking to each other as colleagues rather than enemies. Eventually, they both stood up and wished each other well before heading in opposite directions. Maureen crossed back over the bridge where she stopped briefly, taking a last look at the ducks paddling calmly in the water.

CHAPTER NINE

As Novak knew well, private investigative firms were nearly always hidden in plain sight. A glass-panelled door that led up to a pokey staircase. A name stuck next to a buzzer, alongside those of dentists or massage therapists, or less creditable professions. Often found above shopfronts on empty, scruffy streets that you would only ever discover by accident. The firm belonging to his old friend, Roy Clark, was no different. Tucked away in an unfashionable area of Queens, the front door next to a steel shutter almost completely covered by graffiti.

Novak waited to be buzzed into the building and then made his way up the stairs, finding his way to a dim, chestnut room with worn leather sofas against each wall and a narrow desk where an ageing receptionist sat making notes in a large bound notebook. Her eyes rose from the pages when he came into view and then dipped and rose once more as she registered who he was.

"Mr Novak, is that you?"

"Hello, Beryl. How are you?" said Novak, approaching the desk with a warm smile on his face.

"Goodness, it's been a long time since I've seen you. You're looking very well."

He rested one forearm on the front of the desk, leaning towards her. "As are you. It's as if you're looking younger with each passing year."

Beryl blushed and giggled enthusiastically. Novak smiled, enjoying the satisfaction of flirting with her, before the thought of Maureen's impending meeting with Cassidy came rushing, unwelcome, to his mind.

"I assume you want to see Mr Clark?" she asked.

"Yes please, Beryl. Is he around?"

"He's in his office. Go right in. He'll be delighted to see you."

"Thank you, Beryl." Novak strode past her to the room's only other door.

Knocking once, he twisted the handle and stuck his head inside. A plump and grey-haired man sat in an oversized swivel chair within, wearing an open-collared shirt and flicking through loose papers on the desk in front of him. His broad jaw spread wide when he saw Novak, breaking out into a craterous grin as a deep, southern voice boomed out.

"Bob? You old rascal! What are you doing here?"

He rose from the chair and stuck out his arm to shake Novak's hand.

"Oh, you know. Just passing by."

"What a surprise! Have a seat. Do you want a drink?"

Novak sat down opposite Clark but raised his hand in objection. "No thanks, Roy. I know you; if we have one, that'll be the rest of the day gone."

"How the hell are ya?" said Clark.

"Fine, thank you. And yourself? I see business is still ticking along nicely."

Clark raised his arms wide with a smug smile. "What can I say? I've got no complaints. And what about your firm?"

"I've pretty much stopped working full time. So I can focus on other things."

"I see. What is it? Golf? Fishing? Hunting?"

"Nothing quite as relaxing as that I'm afraid. I've been going through old cases. To sell to newspapers and stuff like that."

"Oh yeah? How's that been working out for you?"

"It keeps me busy."

Clark's face stiffened and his smile disappeared. He suddenly slowed his voice, as if developing a stutter.

"Listen, Bob... We were so sorry to hear about what happened. Really. I tried to call, but I couldn't get hold of you—"

Novak felt the tension start to build in his chest and cut Clark off as soon as he sensed where he was going.

"I know, Roy. I appreciate that. I wasn't taking anyone's calls for a while. I'm sure you can understand."

Clark nodded eagerly and then coughed to clear his throat. An awkwardness filled the room, which Novak elected to break through.

"Listen, Roy, I'm looking for some information on a lead. Does the name Hauptman mean anything to you?"

The smile returned to Clark's face. "Ah here we are. 'Just passing by...'"

Novak stayed firm. "Well?"

"It does, actually," said Clark. "Dirk Hauptman. Big union leader in the fifties. Bit of a scandal at the time."

Novak leant forwards excitedly. "Really? Do you have anything on it?"

Clark scratched his chin and grinned. He eased further into the swivel chair, which squeaked under his weight.

"I might do. What's it worth to you?"

Novak sighed. "Don't worry, you'll get a slice of the pie."

"What kind of pie we talking?"

"About three thousand a slice."

Novak held Clark's gaze for a second. This kind of negotiation was nothing new to either of them, and neither wanted to blink first. Eventually, Clark broke away and nodded, rising from the chair to walk over to a cabinet in the corner of the room.

"Who's interested in old union business? Not very fashionable these days," he said as he searched for the right file.

"Oh, some journalist is putting a book together. I'm just helping them do the legwork."

Clark plucked a brown folder from the cabinet and returned to the desk. "Journalists are a pain in the ass."

Novak chuckled to himself. "Tell me about it."

Clark opened the folder in front of Novak, who began rapidly scanning his eyes over the contents. Clark eagerly summarised what he could remember, now there was a financial reward agreed.

"Like I said, it was a bit of a scandal. All got a bit messy. Started in fifty-nine. You see, the unions in those days had a lot more power and influence than they do now. And some serious backing as well. There was a meeting early that year, in a hotel in Detroit. You can see the clippings of it there."

He pointed to a newspaper photograph on the front page of the file, with around thirty men posing for the camera in a conference room.

"It was a classic old boys' club. Cigars, bourbon, a load of back-slapping. Some of them would even play poker in the background during the discussions. All very casual."

"So what was the problem?"

"There was a disagreement. Hauptman wasn't happy with where they were investing the members' dues."

"Where were they going?"

Clark raised his eyebrows. "Anything that the Mafia had its clutches on at the time."

Novak was intrigued. He knew there had been talk for years of the Mafia's involvement in the labour unions, so it wasn't a complete surprise, but now he was beginning to understand why this case had been kept under wraps for so long.

"So, this Hauptman was a purist then?"

"Exactly," said Clark. "He was a popular guy who had risen

pretty quickly, but yeah, maybe he should have known when to shut his mouth…"

"What happened?"

"He threatened to go to the Feds, made a right stink about it all. So the union bosses had a word with their old mate, Joe Kennedy."

"Why would he help them?"

"To get his kid into office! I told you, the unions had serious power back then. They could swing an election single-handedly."

Novak tried to contain his excitement. This was the link he had been looking for. Maureen had been right; everything was leading back to Kennedy.

"So what happened?"

"I think a quiet word was had with the CIA. And the magic word in those days was communist. You were better off being accused of mass murder than being a red."

"So they arrested Hauptman?"

Clark's face dropped. "They didn't get that far. He jumped out of the window. In front of his wife and kids and everything."

"Jesus."

"I told you this was messy. I guess an idealist like him couldn't stand the idea of being falsely accused."

Novak digested the information quietly for a few moments. He kept looking back to the various documents in Clark's folder. There was a photo of Hauptman, posing for the camera, beaming out a broad, warm smile. His obituary in a local paper. It had started to look like a shrine to a life cut too short.

"How do you have this?" Novak asked Clark.

"I doubt I'm the only one. This is a genuine conspiracy. Everything was covered up. It could've brought down the presidential campaign, as well as airing the union's dirty laundry. People like us live on cases like this."

A thought flashed through Novak's mind. "You don't happen to know the name of any of the CIA agents who were involved?"

"Oh God, now you're testing me," said Clark, drumming his chunky fingers on his temple. "It would have been one of the big shots. Someone close to Kennedy at the time."

"Sean Finn?" offered Novak.

"That's it! That's him!" said Clark noisily.

Novak breathed in sharply. He had found another piece of the puzzle. Finally, after all these years, he was starting to make ground on the investigation. The picture was beginning to get a little clearer. He leant forwards and went to take the folder into his possession. Clark put his hand on top of it, keeping it in place.

"I'm afraid I'm going to need to keep that, Bob. If it's suddenly become of interest after all these years, I wouldn't want to miss the chance to use it again."

Novak smiled through his teeth. He had always known Clark would capitalise on any opportunity that came his way, and begrudgingly admired his shameless love of a cheap payday.

"Fair enough. You've given me plenty."

He rose from his chair and shook Clark's hand firmly.

"I'll wire you the money soon. Nice to see you, Roy."

"And you, Bob."

Novak made his way to the door, Clark following behind to see him out.

"Say hello to Jane for me," Novak said.

"Will do," replied Clark. "Good luck with the investigation. And try not to do this for the rest of your life. It's not too late to get into golf, you know."

Novak laughed and opened the door. "I'll think about it."

CHAPTER TEN

I t had been easy enough to get in touch with Don Cassidy.
Novak had given Maureen his details and she'd phoned him to
arrange a meeting at a restaurant in Washington, under the guise
of him helping her with her research on her new book, *The FBI
Investigations that Changed America*. Even from their brief
encounter over the phone, Novak's warnings about the agent were
clearly justified: Cassidy had spoken in an overtly flirtatious tone,
deliberately pausing and elongating certain words, which he
seemed to think had some kind of seductive effect. Maureen
knew exactly what she was getting herself in for, and prepared
herself accordingly.

The majority of the short flight to the capital had been spent
reflecting on her conversation with Novak on the bench: the
revelations about her father's career in intelligence, the cover-up
of his involvement with Oswald. She thought too about the story
that Marc Randall had told her about the night of JFK's
inauguration. How angry her father had been. The glass smashing
in his hand. What could possibly have happened to make him
hate his former friend so much he was willing to get involved in
the plot to assassinate him?

Halfway through the journey her mind briefly drifted to an unexpected destination and Maureen found herself smiling as she recalled Novak's awkwardness in explaining the Cassidy plan. He had essentially admitted that he was aware of her attractiveness, enough to use it as a weapon in the investigation, but she wasn't sure if that extended as far as him recognising, or even admiring, that attractiveness himself. Had that been on his mind from their first meeting? Maureen shook the thought away and stared back out of the window, forcing herself to refocus on the more pressing issues.

After landing, she booked herself into a hotel room and spent the few hours she had to herself, before meeting Cassidy later that evening, relaxing and taking her time getting ready. It was as she lay bathing in the small and simple hotel tub that she realised she couldn't remember the last time she had put so much effort into going on a "date". One of her more expensive dresses had been chosen for the occasion, a sparkling black and gold number, and as she carefully applied her make-up in the mirror, she stopped at regular intervals to closely inspect her appearance.

"Not bad," was the verdict that she mouthed back at her reflection, the words forming between pursed, red lips.

To complete the outfit, she scooped up a leather clutch bag that had been a luxury present to herself after one of her royalty cheques had come through, and matched that with Karl Lagerfeld heels. The hotel reception called her a cab and she took some satisfaction that the spotty young bellboy couldn't stop himself from stealing glances at her while she waited.

The restaurant that Cassidy had chosen was called Moby Joe's, on a fashionable and packed street in a vibrant, multicultural neighbourhood of the city. Maureen noticed eateries and bars of different cuisines following one after the other as she stared out of the taxi window. There were groups of people talking and smoking in the streets and bright, twinkling lights above every front window. As they approached the restaurant, she saw a line of at least ten expensive, immaculate cars parked up, waiting for the valet service. There was a ruby-red veranda protruding out of a large, square building, with the name displayed in a cartoonish font on the fabric. Men in suits and white jackets waited below it, intermittently opening the door as the guests arrived.

Maureen joined the line of diners to the side of the veranda and watched as one by one they were admitted inside. When it was her turn, the maître d' greeted her with a warm smile and she shyly stated that she thought she had a reservation.

"I believe the table is under Mr Cassidy's name."

The man reacted instantaneously and extended his arm to guide her through the entrance. "Of course, you'll be seated at Mr Cassidy's favourite table. He will be along shortly, I am sure."

Maureen smiled, but couldn't help notice the slight hint of pity or judgement that sneaked across the man's face. She wondered how often Cassidy entertained female guests at Moby Joe's and what character of woman the staff had come to expect.

A succession of doors were opened for her before she found herself in the main room of the restaurant. She paused for a moment to take it in. The main lights of the room had been dimmed to such an extent, they essentially ceased to serve a purpose, yet it was glimmeringly bright inside. This was due to a series of candelabras and lanterns placed on each round table, resting atop the white silk cloths that adorned them. Their light shimmered on the cutlery and reflected upwards and around the giant space, before being caught in the reflection of five enormous, wall-length mirrors and in the numerous bulbs of a dazzling crystal chandelier. The tables had been arranged in a circle, with a space left in the centre of the room, and guests were crammed tightly together, each within touching distance of the table in front and behind. There was a raised platform in one corner, where a full swing band was playing energetically. It was loud and lively and overwhelming all at once. Maureen felt as if she had been transported back to a jazz club in the sixties. She half expected Frank Sinatra or Dean Martin to stride out from the narrow gaps in the seating and begin to sing in the vacant central space.

A waiter softly touched her elbow. "If you'd like to follow me, madame?"

He led her to a table near the middle of the restaurant's concentric layout and pulled out the chair for her, waiting for her to sit down before departing. Maureen felt the eyes of the patrons at the nearest tables upon her as she sat, and looked nervously down at her cutlery. It had become clear that Cassidy had deliberately made sure she would arrive first, saving the grand entrance for himself.

And sure enough, a few minutes later, he did just that. Maureen became aware of a man striding towards her at pace from a few tables away, a wide and mischievous smile on his face. He was well dressed, in a tailored navy suit with a black tie, and had an olive hue to his skin that Maureen guessed was the product of a tanning bed. Her first impression of him was of a man who had done everything possible to fight his age. There was an unmistakeable grey tint in his slick, combed-back hair, while his face had been preened so that there wasn't a stray follicle around his nose and eyebrows, which gave him an intense, clown-like quality as he beamed at her. As she stood to greet him, she saw that he was a couple of inches taller than her, even in her heels, and that he had broad, square shoulders that bulked out over his chest.

"Maureen Finn! It's a pleasure," said Cassidy, in a velvety East Coast accent.

"Mr Cassidy, so nice to meet you," she said, extending her hand.

"Put that away!" he said, lightly swiping her hand to the side and leaning across her body to plant a moist kiss on her cheek. Maureen was thrown off guard, but chuckled politely.

He pointed, indicating she should sit, and then took the seat opposite her, reclining immediately and allowing his gaze to admire all of the room.

"What do you think of the place, huh?"

"I like it, it's got real–" started Maureen, but Cassidy immediately interrupted her, sticking a hand out towards a nearby waiter.

"Pepe! We'll have two glasses of champagne when you're ready, please."

The waiter hadn't been attending to them but was quick to respond. "Of course, Mr Cassidy, right away."

Maureen silently seethed. She hated being interrupted or ignored, especially in the outrageously brash way Cassidy had just done. Reminding herself what she had come to Washington for, she forced a smile back onto her lips.

"I want to thank you for agreeing to meet with me at such short notice."

"Please. I'm always available for dinner with a beautiful woman," he said, letting his eyes run clumsily down from her chin and drift all over her body.

The glasses of champagne arrived with incredible speed and Cassidy thanked the waiter, Maureen noticing him slip a twenty-dollar bill into the man's hand as he left them.

"So, what can I help you with exactly?" asked Cassidy, taking a sip from his glass.

"As you know, my latest book is about the most important FBI investigations of recent decades. I need to get as much information as possible, but as you can imagine, your organisation is a tough nut to crack when it comes to accessing records."

"Well, as I'm sure you can appreciate, the FBI has to maintain a tough line when it comes to protecting our archives," he started formally, before lowering his voice. "Though there are always ways of getting inside the fence."

"I'd be so grateful for anything you could give me," said Maureen, looking up at Cassidy flirtatiously.

He smirked to himself, but returned to his champagne. "What period are you interested in?"

"The cold war mainly. Specifically the fifties."

"Ah, the good old days. I've certainly got a few stories I can tell you about back then."

"Fantastic," Maureen replied. "What was your main role during that time?"

"Mainly surveillance. Nothing super exciting, but everyone has to start somewhere, of course. And I think my bosses could tell I was itching for more responsibility, that I had something to offer, so pretty quickly I was put in charge of some high-profile cases. Some big-name Commies," he said, with the evident assumption this would impress her.

"Oh really? How did that come about?" asked Maureen, already knowing the answer.

"There was a guy before me who quit. Couldn't handle the job anymore apparently, so they got someone in to clean up his mess."

Sensing an opportunity to amuse herself, Maureen asked: "Who was that? The guy who couldn't handle it?"

"Novak, his name was. Robert Novak. He just wasn't up to the Bureau standards."

"What was Novak like?" said Maureen, unable to resist.

"Straight as an arrow. And about as much fun as a bullet in the leg. I could never quite work him out."

Maureen nodded, enjoying the character reference. A different waiter appeared with a notepad and asked them for their order, which confused Maureen as she hadn't even seen a menu yet.

"I'll have the lobster, Carl. Maureen, you like lobster? It's phenomenal here."

"Uh, sure," said Maureen, not really certain she had any other choice.

"That's two lobsters then," said Cassidy, patting the waiter on the back as he departed.

Returning to the line of conversation, Maureen asked, "You said that you had some high-profile cases? Anyone I'd know."

Cassidy scoffed. "Hell, yeah. You'd know them all right."

Maureen raised her eyebrows suggestively. "Go on then, I dare you to name one."

Cassidy laughed dismissively. "I'm not that easy, sweetheart."

"Oh come on, impress me."

Cassidy leant forwards. "Fine, heard of Boris Starkov?"

Maureen shook her head in exaggerated disappointment. "Nope."

"Beretsky?"

"No idea. Come on, you must have someone more famous than that."

Cassidy's face flashed red. Maureen had successfully managed to provoke him.

"Okay then, how about Lee Harvey Oswald then? Heard of him?"

Maureen feigned a dramatic sense of shock, staggering back in her chair. This delighted Cassidy and he returned to his default smug and sanctimonious demeanour.

"No, really?" said Maureen.

"Big time. And let me tell you, there's a lot more to the story than you'd believe. The public don't know the half of it."

Maureen now sprang forwards, sitting at the edge of her chair to convey her enthusiasm, making sure she put her hand on Cassidy's side of the table. She was surprised by just how easy it had been to get the agent to thoughtlessly brag about strictly confidential information.

"Now, you simply have to tell me more about that."

"Not a chance," he replied. "They'd have my head for giving up the truth about that one."

Maureen sensed that she had one last option available to her and decided to go for it. Her fingers edged off the silk of the table and wandered along the top of Cassidy's hand, delicately touching the metal of his watch and then the skin of his wrist. She tried to make herself look as vulnerable and desperate as she could manage.

"I'm going to tell you the truth. I know that my father worked in intelligence and was somehow involved in a conspiracy around the Kennedy assassination. It's killing me that a man I looked up to might have given up his country. I just want to find out what happened and I would do... anything to get the information I need."

Cassidy's smirk turned more sinister as he grabbed her hand and squeezed it tightly in his palm. "I understand your pain, Maureen, and I want to do everything I can to help. I have some files back in my apartment. After dinner, why don't we go and see what we can find?"

Maureen felt a chill come over her. Novak had been right. Cassidy was going to stop at nothing to fulfil his intentions for the evening, and whatever hopes she'd had of extracting everything at the restaurant was going to be impossible. If she wanted to find the information she needed, she was going to have to go back to the dragon's lair.

Gulping down her repulsion, she muttered softly, "That sounds like a good idea."

The evening returned to a more casual tone. The lobster was brought out and Cassidy attacked his rapaciously, sucking the meat from the bones with a slurp and picking at the shells for any remainders. It made Maureen shudder to watch him ravage the lobster's flesh, reminding her of the price she might have to pay to get what she wanted from their meeting. She ate more slowly, but did have to admit that it was delicious. Conversation became more difficult when a singer, a middle-aged woman with umber skin and a long emerald dress entered the central space and began to sing soft, melodic classics barely a few feet away from them. At times, she even came right up to their table, taking Maureen's hand in hers and smiling sympathetically at her. She wondered what the singer was trying to tell her through her smoky, black eyes.

Once their plates had been cleared and Cassidy had polished off his third glass of champagne, he sighed loudly and asked, "So, you still want to find out more about your father?"

"Of course. Anything you have would be invaluable."

"Then let's get out of here. My place isn't far."

Maureen followed him out of Moby Joe's, waiting impatiently as he made a show of thanking all the staff and bidding various regulars goodbye. He handled himself like a Mafia boss, making sure that everyone in the room knew he was some kind of big shot. Once they were out front, there was a taxi already waiting and the back door was opened for Maureen. It was such a remarkably efficient process that she realised that Cassidy must have gradually perfected it over time. She found herself thinking of the other poor women who had fallen victim to his sleazy wine and dine operations.

He slid in to join her in the back seat and barked an instruction at the driver. Maureen felt his hand slide onto her thigh as the car began to pull away from the restaurant, gripping her flesh just below the line of her dress. She elected to try and ignore it as best she could, looking out at the Washington scenery as a distraction.

Cassidy hadn't lied; his apartment was no more than five or six blocks away from the restaurant, on a clean, fashionable and expensive-looking street made up of short and quirky terraced houses that were all painted different colours, with maple trees lining the pavements outside. The streetlights caused the leaves of the trees to cast shadows onto the fronts of the dwellings and gave the place an eerie quality, as if stolen from the scenes of a classic film noir.

Cassidy had a first-floor apartment and he led Maureen up a small staircase before opening the door and gesturing her to go inside. She was led to a spacious open-plan living room, decorated in purple striped wallpaper that resembled pyjama material, with a space left for an old fireplace. An oak dining table was tucked into the corner closest to the kitchen. The rest of the space was dominated by large leather sofas and a desk placed in front of a bookcase that held no books, but instead dozens of boxes and binders stacked unevenly on top of each other. This was where the files on her father would be, Maureen thought.

"Can I get you a drink? I have brandy," said Cassidy, the champagne having reduced his voice to an almost ludicrous low slur.

"Sure," said Maureen, her eyes still on the bookcase.

He retreated to another corner, this one containing a small wooden unit that looked like a kind of coffee table, until Cassidy lifted a handle and the top layer rose to reveal a bar cart, containing all kinds of spirits within. He filled two rocks glasses and returned to hand one to Maureen, before he sinuously positioned himself behind her, so she could smell his breath permeating her neck, and started to slowly run his hand through the lowest strands of her hair.

"You really are something, Maureen, you know," he said in a soft hiss.

"Thank you," choked Maureen, beginning to sweat.

"Now, if I'm going to give you information about your father... what are you going to give me?"

Maureen realised with horror that he was reaching for the zipper at the top of her dress. She reacted quickly, turning on her heel to face him and knocking his hand away. Then, she grabbed his tie and made sure she looked seductively into his eyes and then down to his lips, biting her own.

"I've got an idea of how we can work that out," she whispered.

Pushing him gently towards the dining table, she began unfastening his tie. He smiled and breathed out in stilted moans as she pulled out the nearest chair and then pushed him hard down onto it. She took his glass from his hand and placed it on the table, alongside hers. As he once more groped for her, she took the tie off his neck and wrapped it around his arms, tying them to the back of the chair.

"Oh, you're not your average girl, are you? You're trouble," said Cassidy, in evident delight.

Maureen made sure she tied the knot as tight as she could, ensuring he couldn't squirm out of the hold, and then stepped back a few paces, looking at him suggestively once again.

"Here's the deal then. For every piece of information you give me, I take off an item of clothing. How does that sound?"

Cassidy was agog with desire and excitement. "Sounds fair to me," he gasped.

"Okay then." Maureen took a moment to ensure she was asking the right questions. "Now I know my father worked for the CIA during the period, but what was his reputation back then?"

Cassidy didn't even look up at her face, his eyes resting along the edges of her dress. "He was incredibly highly regarded, of course. A name that everyone knew, and a lot of people feared. He had worked in Europe during the height of the war and there were rumours he had been involved in prisoner exchanges. Really high-level stuff. And then..."

He stopped himself and flashed that smug, manic grin up at her, as if to suggest that it was her turn.

"Oh no, that's not enough. What happened next?" said Maureen.

"He had a fall out with the hierarchy. I don't know what it was about. And then he quit the service in disgrace in nineteen sixty." Cassidy's tone suggested he knew he was already giving too much away.

"Okay, very good," said Maureen, teasingly. And with that, she raised her leg and slowly worked one of her heels off the base of her foot, so it dangled briefly on her toes. With that, she flicked her leg and sent the shoe skidding along the floor towards Cassidy. He squirmed and moaned in submissive glee.

Maureen continued her questioning, turning her attention to the bookcase. "Do you have his file here?"

Cassidy shook his head. "No. That's one file I would never have been allowed to take home with me."

Intrigued at this, Maureen pushed further. "Well, I hope your memory's good then, otherwise it looks like I'll be staying exactly as I am."

Cassidy paused for a moment, clearly considering whether he should stop this dangerous game altogether, but he was now no more than a slave to his own lust and he relented once more. "I do remember something. There was a photo of Sean Finn meeting with a Soviet agent. In the Presidential Library in New York. A few months before the assassination of Kennedy."

Maureen began rolling the heel off her other foot but kept it suspended as she asked, "What agent? Give me his name."

"Tambov. Victor Tambov. He was one of the most notorious KGB operatives."

Maureen kicked the heel off. She knew she was finally getting somewhere, but also that she was running out of clothes.

"Tell me more about this Tambov. Why did my father meet with him?"

"I don't know."

"Do you have a file on Tambov?" asked Maureen.

Cassidy's eyes briefly but unmistakably flickered over to the bookcase, answering her question.

"Aha," said Maureen. "Now you're going to tell me which one."

"And why on earth would I do that?"

Maureen sighed to herself but knew what she needed to do to seal the deal. She turned so that she was facing away from Cassidy and then swept her hair to one side, placing her hand on the top of her zipper and slowly pulling it down, only to the bottom of her shoulder blades, but enough so that the strap of her bra became visible to him.

"If you want me to keep going, you'll point out the file."

Cassidy had begun to resemble a torture victim. He was sweating profusely and chewing vigorously on the bottom of his lip, in the manner of a scolded schoolboy. He was trapped between what he longed for and knowing he was giving up valuable secrets, and the inner conflict was visibly overwhelming him.

Maureen stayed turned away, keeping the exposed skin of her back to him, waiting patiently for the words she craved.

Finally, in a defeated whimper, Cassidy muttered, "Third shelf up. Second binder from the right."

Maureen repressed her delight at knowing that victory was finally hers. She strode purposefully straight to the shelf, located the binder and pushed it open. Inside was a collection of grey-lined, laminated folders, with the names of the subjects typed in the top right corners. After a moment or so she spotted Tambov's name and withdrew the folder from its home.

Cassidy had grown even more agitated and was shuffling his feet along the floor. "We can look through it after we're done. Now, for heaven's sake, take off that goddamn dress!"

Maureen turned towards him, fixing him with a stoic, paralysing stare. She walked slowly towards him, his frustrated struggles coming to an immediate halt. As she was no more than a foot away from him, she returned her hand to the top of her spine, locating the zipper between her fingers.

"No," she said in a cutting, emotionless whisper, before re-zipping the top of her dress and retrieving her heels from the floor beside him.

Cassidy's face dropped as it finally occurred to him that he had been well and truly outplayed, and his desperate, lustful excitement was replaced with a burning rage. The chair shook furiously as he tried to wrestle himself free.

Maureen tucked Tambov's folder into her bag and placed her shoes back on her feet. Taking one last look at the pitiful scene as the agent began to scream obscenities at her at the top of his voice, she offered him a final line to remember her by.

"Goodbye, Mr Cassidy. Thank you for dinner. The lobster really was phenomenal."

CHAPTER ELEVEN

Novak made one more stop before he headed back to his apartment for the evening. There was a dry-cleaners just around the corner from his home in Brooklyn: Russo's, where he had been going for years. It was a dark and drizzly night and the neon lights of the street sparkled in the rain as he approached. He was running late, so walked swiftly, pushing his way past slower pedestrians on the sidewalk. When he reached the door of the cleaners, he went to push open the door but found it locked. He looked pleadingly inside and could see that the lights were still on and that Mr Russo himself was still behind the counter. Novak breathed a sigh of relief as the owner came to open the door.

"I'm so sorry, Mr Russo. I was running late."

"Not a problem, Mr Novak. For you, we are always open," the small, wrinkled man replied.

"I just wondered if you'd had a chance to do my coat. The black Chesterfield?"

Novak was allowed to step out of the rain and onto the carpet of the store, but Russo stayed with him at the entrance, responding to his request with a look of confusion.

"I thought we had delivered it to you earlier today, Mr

Novak."

Now it was Novak's turn to look bemused. "What? I haven't been home all day."

Russo beckoned to Novak to follow him as he headed to the counter, opening the till and flicking through a series of paper receipts that had been stabbed onto a silver spindle. Novak waited patiently and after a few moments Russo exclaimed and pulled one of the papers from the pile to show him.

"Yes. See. This is you. Chesterfield coat. Mr Novak. 37th Street."

He handed Novak the receipt so he could look for himself and sure enough the paper listed all the information exactly as Russo described it, with a time earlier that very afternoon. The same time that Novak had been with Roy Clark in his office in Queens.

"Well I promise I wasn't there to receive it. Did you leave it by the door?"

Russo snickered. "Not in this neighbourhood; we always make sure the customer is in."

"Who does the deliveries?"

"My nephew mainly. He's still here, I think. One moment."

Russo walked over to an open doorway to the right of the till, partly hidden by hanging beads. He yelled through the doorway without crossing the threshold.

"Hey, Frankie! You know Mr Novak's coat? You did deliver it this afternoon, right?"

A teenage voice came back. "Yeah. Why?"

"Well he's here now and he says he wasn't at home today, so you definitely handed it to someone?"

"I knocked on the door, asked for Mr Novak, a guy opened the door and took the coat. What more can I do?"

Novak's mind was already spinning as they exchanged words. His experience in his line of work had given him a sense for when something seemed off and he was already planning his next move. Getting his coat was now the least of his worries.

Russo came back over to him. "Well there you have it. It's the problem with kids these days, they don't question anything. If it's not there when you get home, I'll reimburse you for your troubles of course–"

Novak interrupted him. "No need. Neither you nor your nephew have done anything wrong. I've been expecting a visit from my cousin from Canada. I'm sure he's just arrived a few days early."

"So, all is fine?" said Russo uncertainly.

"Yes, it's all fine."

Russo looked like he wanted to say something else, but lowered his head instead, his desire to get home for the evening defeating his curiosity.

"Goodnight, Mr Russo. I'm sorry to have kept you later."

Novak walked back out onto the street with an acute sense of alertness. He looked around him, scanning his surroundings. Then, when he was satisfied, he headed for a side street, where he knew there was a telephone booth. He ducked inside, grateful to be out of the rain. He slipped some quarters into the machine and held the receiver to his ear. After he had dialled the number, he waited for the response at the other end.

"911. What's your emergency?"

"Hi, yes. I think my apartment has been broken into."

"Okay, sir. Are you in the apartment now?"

"No. I'm calling from outside."

"Okay. If you could give me the address, please."

"588 North 37th Street. Fifth Floor. I'm number 42."

"Okay, sir. And do you have any information on the potential intruders?"

"I heard voices as I was about to go in, there seemed to be a few of them. Please hurry, I'm very afraid."

"Okay. Please stay in a safe place, we will be sending officers over right away."

"Thank you."

Novak thrust the phone back in the holder and took a minute to himself, his nerves still on edge. He forced himself to calm down and thought of the logical next steps, before the idea came to him. There was a café right across the road from his apartment that was always open late. That would give him the best view of whatever was about to unfold.

He left the booth and walked calmly back to his own street, wincing and blinking away the rain that occasionally splattered in his eyes. Scaloni's was open as he'd expected and there were still a couple of tables filled with people getting something to eat. The anticipation had unsettled Novak's stomach so he just ordered black coffee and seated himself at a table in the window, offering him the best possible view of the front door of his building opposite.

The minutes ticked by, as Novak gripped both sides of the mug to warm his hands, unable to take his mind anywhere but the impending events in his apartment. After a few minutes, a police car arrived and parked haphazardly on the sidewalk outside the front door. Two officers stepped out and entered the building. Novak clutched the mug tighter still.

The time ticked by, with Novak's gaze fixed on the front entrance. And then the officers re-emerged. This time they were not alone. Each was leading a man in front of them, his hands handcuffed tightly behind his back. Novak focused on the men's faces as intensely as he could. Both were of athletic build and wearing smart clothes, but he didn't recognise them. The one at the front was talking a lot, clearly arguing with the officers, but Novak couldn't make out what he was saying.

He waited, watching the two men being put in the back of the police car. His suspicions had been correct. It gave him a mixed sensation, an undeniable sense of satisfaction, not least at the inconvenience and embarrassment he had just caused his unwelcome visitors, but tinged with a sense of fear. He now knew that his apartment, his home, was no longer safe.

After he was certain the coast was clear, he left Scaloni's and made his way across the street to his building. He took the stairs all the way up to his floor, still constantly checking around to see if he was being followed. When he reached his front door, he approached tentatively, listening in before he put the key in the lock, even though all the evidence was that whoever had been there had been rather unceremoniously removed. The door opened and Novak caught the first glimpse of what had happened to his home.

Everything was open. The cupboards in the kitchen, the drawers in various side tables, the doors to his bedroom and bathroom. There were upturned pictures and documents scattered all over the coffee table. He could make out everything from bank statements to letters he had exchanged with old friends. All the lights were on. Novak crossed the room quickly, pushing past the television to a slot in the wall where his safe was located. He tried to move the lock, relieved to find it was still shut. Immediately he moved to the mantelpiece, taking the picture of his children in his hands. He turned it around and grasped at the stand until the wood came loose. Pressed against the back of the photograph was a small metal key, which he took out of the frame.

Returning to the safe, he placed the key in the lock and the door swung open with a click. He retrieved a clear bag of rolled-up notes, his passport and a couple of documents, all in narrow brown envelopes. He put them in a rucksack with a few changes of clothes and then zipped it up, slinging it over his shoulder. The last thing he did was pick up the picture frame, returning the wood to its back so it could stand upright once more. Placing it on the mantelpiece again, he smiled back at the beaming faces of his children. And then he turned on his heel and strode straight out of the apartment, flicking the light switch as he passed and noting, still in the plastic of the dry-cleaning bag, his black Chesterfield coat thrown carelessly over the arm of the sofa.

CHAPTER TWELVE

Maureen caught the next available flight out of Washington. She felt the rush to leave the city from the second she stepped out of Cassidy's apartment, knowing that her actions towards the FBI agent had placed a target on her back. Despite her eagerness to open up the folder she had stolen, the sense of danger meant that she resisted, deciding to save it until she was safely back within the confines of her own home.

She decided to catch a taxi for the final leg of the journey and started to fantasise about changing into comfortable clothes and putting her feet up on her sofa. The moment the taxi pulled up outside her building, she paid the fare and jumped out.

Her apartment building was made up of five floors and had a limited but pleasant lobby with a welcome mat and a set of lockers where mail was delivered, located immediately to the right of the front door. It was deserted, which pleased her, as she didn't have the energy to engage in small talk with her neighbours. Her final task before finally entering her own space was to check to see if she had any mail. She twisted the small key in the lock of her mailbox.

At that moment she became aware of a sudden presence

behind her, a figure moving at startling speed. It was too late for
her to turn around as a firm arm was thrown around her neck, the
palm of a weathered hand thrust over her mouth. Maureen's
attempt to scream was stifled immediately as fear and panic filled
her body.

Was it Cassidy? How had he managed to find her so quickly?
Or was it another FBI contact who had been alerted to her theft
of private documents?

The answer was revealed quickly enough. "Would you stop
struggling, please?" said the familiar measured tone of Novak.

She relaxed slightly, but was still confused and restless. He
gradually released his fingers so that she could speak, but his arm
stayed coiled around her throat.

"What are you doing?"

"Who did you tell about the investigation?"

"What?" Maureen was apoplectic, her tiredness and
adrenaline mixed into an all-consuming anger.

Novak's tone didn't waver. "I know you gave me up. Who did
you tell?"

"Are you out of your mind?" She swung her arms madly to try
to create some distance between them. As her elbow grazed his
chin, Novak finally released his hold. Now they were finally facing
each other she could make out his appearance. He looked as if he
hadn't slept; Maureen noticed the first signs of stubble breaking
out on his chin and along his jaw. His eyes bore into her skull,
filled with suspicion.

"Do you want to tell me what the hell is going on?"

"Follow me," he said emptily, ignoring her entirely and walking
straight past.

She sighed. He could never just answer the question.
Nonetheless, she traipsed behind him diligently, her bemusement
growing as he left the lobby by the front door and ducked down
an alley that led around the back of the building, where there was
nothing but the garbage cans. There was smashed glass on the

ground and a pair of small, scrawny birds landed on the tops of the bins intermittently. As they finally came to a stop, Novak spoke in hushed tones.

"We're being tracked," he said. "They tried to catch me in New York."

Maureen's face dropped. "How did you get out?"

"Luck," he replied dryly. "And believe it or not, I haven't encountered any issues with people breaking into my home until you came along."

"You're accusing me of betraying you?" she said with disgust.

"Who else is there?" he yelled back.

"I haven't said a word to anyone!" Maureen retaliated, nostrils flaring. "Honestly, after everything I've done for this investigation, this is how I'm thanked. By being assaulted in my own home!"

Novak's shoulders sank and he leant back on his heel, his eyes leaving Maureen's and searching aimlessly along the ground. For the first time, she could sense that he was starting to believe her, and that guilt was beginning to replace his wild sense of injustice.

"Then who else could it be? How do they know about our plans?"

"I don't know!" cried Maureen, running her fingers roughly over her eyes.

Novak fell quiet, breathing heavily. He had looked almost deranged at first, but this had been replaced by a drained and defeated countenance, as if the air had been sucked from him.

He spoke in a sombre murmur. "Well, we can't say that we haven't tried. But we just don't have enough. No evidence, no witness, nothing. And the people we're up against... we're swimming against the tide."

Maureen opened her arms irritably. "So?"

"Better to give up before it's too late."

"Are you serious?!"

"Look, your father's reputation is still intact. Isn't that what you wanted?"

Maureen turned away from him, throwing out a hand in disgust. "You're such a coward! All this, everything you've put me through and you give up at the first hurdle?" She paused before delivering her final jab. "Your father would be ashamed of you."

The jibe sparked Novak into life. Colour returned to his face and his eyes flashed with anger as he snapped back at her. "You entitled little brat. You know nothing about me, about my father! I'm just trying to keep you safe, because unlike you I know just how dangerous this situation is."

"Oh, and keeping me safe meant sending me to meet Cassidy?" said Maureen, her eyes wide and unblinking.

That seemed to disarm Novak, who appeared to have forgotten everything from their last meeting. "You saw him then? How did it go?"

Maureen turned away from him. "What do you care?"

"You're such a child."

"At least I don't give up at the first sign of trouble."

"Trouble? This isn't just a little hiccup, Maureen, this means we are being followed by highly trained agents. Who could have us both put in prison whenever they so choose."

He had strayed closer to her, and by the end he was yelling directly into her face. Maureen could feel the warmth of his breath as she stared unflinchingly back at him. They stayed like that for a moment, locked in a face-off, until finally Novak broke away defeatedly once more.

"Isn't that just further proof that what we're investigating is important?" said Maureen, dictating to him, thrusting her hands out.

"Listen, if we had more to go on, I would continue, I really would," he replied.

"We do," said Maureen. "I stole a file from Cassidy's apartment. He told me that my father met with a Soviet agent before the assassination, and I have his record in my bag at this very moment."

Novak perked up once more, looking at her as if to check she was being serious. Maureen kept her lips pursed and her jaw clenched. Her limbs were tight with tension.

"How did you do that?"

"Magic," said Maureen. "The kind of magic that only women possess."

She could see a flash of jealousy in Novak's reaction, but he hid it well, gritting his teeth behind his lips.

"Let's go up to my apartment."

"No. If they bugged mine, they've almost certainly bugged yours too."

"Then we'll have to stay quiet. I see that only as a bonus," said Maureen and she set off back up the alley, enjoying the fact she was now the one making him follow.

They walked up to her apartment in silence and stayed that way even after Maureen had opened the door. It appeared more or less the same as she had left it but there was something about it that appeared off. She wondered if that was just her paranoia after what Novak had told her or if it was some instinct about her own home.

They went over to sit at her table, where Maureen emptied her bag onto the surface. She opened the laminated folder and the two of them began scanning its contents. It consisted of a series of pages filled with neat rows of typed sentences, the pages marked by random and infrequent scribbles of initials in the corners and blank spaces between the paragraphs and photos.

The opening lines gave a loose background on the subject, Victor Tambov, including his date of birth, dates of his service with the KGB and the various operations he had been involved in. Attached to this, with a paper clip, was a mugshot of Tambov. He was a narrow-faced man with wild eyebrows and a large, creased forehead. His most striking feature was his wide, bright eyes. The details typed on the page, with an occasional handwritten amendment, revealed the information they were after:

> *Victor Tambov was a leading KGB agent during the fifties and early sixties. Worked under the guise of an international chess player for many years, winning many tournaments. Tambov known to have been one of the agents with ties to Lee Harvey Oswald, with eyewitness accounts of them meeting before Oswald's return to the United States. Tambov suspected to have led the theft of private government documents in 1962. Left the KGB in 1970 and relocated to Kiev.*

Maureen looked up once she had scanned through the first page. Novak did the same and the two shared a glance, each raising their eyebrows in the other's direction.

The next page showed a different photo, this one not posed but instead showing Tambov with the instantly recognisable figure of Maureen's father, which gave her a sudden jolt in her stomach. He and the Russian sat on opposite sides of a long wooden table, with a set of large bookshelves in the background. Both their faces were pointed downwards. Once more, there were notes underneath:

> *Sean Finn was caught meeting with Victor Tambov at the FDR Presidential Library, in Hyde Park, NY State, in April 1963.*

Maureen finished reading and waited for Novak to do the

same. He lifted his eyes from the photographs and the two of them sat facing each other, maintaining their silence. An idea came to Maureen and she rose abruptly from the table, pacing across the room to where she kept an antique, bronze record player that had been a gift from an aunt when she had turned twenty-one. She picked a record out of the small collection beside it and placed her chosen vinyl onto the base, lowering the stylus slowly. A few seconds passed and then the loud strains of an orchestra bellowed out into the room, followed by the booming voice of an opera singer.

Maureen went back over to the table and drew her chair closer to Novak's, so there was no more than a few inches between their knees. He gave her a nod of understanding and the two of them began to whisper to each other.

Listening attentively to the music, Novak mused, "'The Coronation of Poppea'?"

Maureen nodded, impressed. "I didn't have you down as an opera fan."

Novak chuckled. "I think we'll start to get along a lot better when we stop underestimating each other." His eyes flickered towards the photographs on the table.

Maureen fell silent for a moment, processing her thoughts before saying them out loud.

"This meeting with Tambov, the KGB agent. Leaving the CIA how he did. It all points to one thing. You don't think... he was a defector to the Soviets, do you?"

Novak shook his head. "I can't believe that. He was the biggest patriot there was, your father. There must be more to it than that."

Maureen was distracted once more by the picture of her father that hung above them, his eyes bearing down on her. His hat tucked under his arm. His uniform pristine. The perfect image of a man who would never let down his country, let alone betray it. Maureen was growing less and less sure of that by the second.

She forced her mind back into focus. "This Tambov, you don't think he could be Clipper, do you?"

Novak shrugged. "I have no idea, but he's the best lead we've got." He stopped and corrected himself. "Or our only one anyway."

"Do you think we'll be able to find him?"

"It won't be easy. And it's certainly going to be impossible to find anything on him here. We'll have to go to Kiev."

The observation caused them both to pause and reflect. Each of them knew this was the reality and their only chance of continuing the investigation, but there was a mutual sense of solemnity that their journey was now about to lead them out of the country and deep into the Eastern Bloc, an area of the world that had, until very recently, seemed a restricted and un-breachable area of the globe, and never to be visited by Americans.

"It will be difficult to get there," mused Maureen.

"But not impossible," replied Novak, raising an eyebrow.

"What about whoever's tracking us? They're not exactly going to willingly let us leave the country."

"I know. We're going to have to cover our tracks."

An idea struck Maureen once more and she raised a finger. She returned to the record player and paused the sounds of the opera, filling the room once again with silence. Crossing the room, she picked up her phone and dialled a number, waiting patiently for an answer. When it came, she made sure to speak as loudly and clearly as she could.

"Hi, Mom. It's me."

Her mother's enthused tones came down the line. "Maureen, sweetheart! I haven't heard from you since I saw you the other night, are you all right?"

"Yes, Mom. I'm fine. Just wanted to see if I could come for dinner on Monday?"

"Of course! You know you don't even have to ask..."

"Thanks, Mom."

"Are you sure everything's okay, sweetheart?" asked her mother.

"I'm just tired. It's been a long few days. Need to sleep."

"Okay, but don't use those dreadful sleeping pills though, please. I don't trust them."

Maureen laughed wearily. "I won't, Mom, I promise."

"Okay, sweetheart. I'll see you Monday. I love you."

"Love you too, Mom." Maureen put the phone down on the table.

The sound of the line cutting out echoed across a small office in FBI headquarters in Washington. Two men were listening intently, headphones over their ears, scribbling notes onto large white pads in front of them. A tape recorder rolled around and around in the centre of the table. They waited a few moments after the call had ended before the first man pushed the headphones back and spoke to his colleague.

"I thought she was going to say something more interesting than that."

The second man shrugged. "Still, it's a plan of some kind. Go and tell the boss. He'll want to know."

CHAPTER THIRTEEN

Maureen packed up belongings for the trip while Novak stood waiting, facing her bookshelf. She ignored his silent judgement of her collection as she stuffed her passport, documents and a book she had recently purchased on the collapse of the Soviet Union on top of a handful of clothes that she had retrieved from her bedroom.

They grabbed something to eat nearby and set about formulating their plan to get to Kiev undetected. Maureen elected to avoid the cafés she normally frequented for fear that they would be monitored, so instead chose a weary-looking Chinese restaurant on the corner of a backstreet, that she passed nearly every day but had never previously entered. There was only one other occupied table so they sat away from the window and ordered herbal tea and a few plates to share. Novak ate greedily and unapologetically, his appetite returning to him after his rapid departure from New York. The service was disinterested and almost entirely absent, which was ideal, giving them a quiet shelter to discuss their ideas.

"What's your plan?" asked Novak.

"Well, I'm guessing it's too risky to fly so we need to find another way out of the country for a start."

"They'll track our cards. Best to use cash."

"What about if we went by sea?"

Novak grimaced. "That'll take weeks."

"Okay, well we could rent a car and head for the border?"

"The rental companies have to keep personal details for their records. They'll give us up as soon as they're asked."

This prompted minutes of silence, as the two of them ate, both frantically scanning through any other options in their minds. As she was just about to finish her vegetable spring rolls, Maureen suddenly slapped the table enthusiastically. "I've got it." She looked at Novak intently. "Are you carrying any cheques?"

As it happened, Novak was. He had packed some in his hastily arranged luggage so that he could pay Roy Clark for the information on Dirk Hauptman, even if he had to do it from afar. He withdrew the chequebook from his bag and stretched it out in front of Maureen.

"Write one out to me. For two thousand dollars."

He was clearly totally bemused. "What? Are you kidding?"

She laughed at him patronisingly. "I'm not charging you a fee, dummy. Your bank is in New York, right? Which means that cheque has to get there before it can be cleared, but I can cash it immediately."

He began to understand what she was getting at and followed her instructions, writing down her details on the first slip of paper. He signed the back and then handed it over to her begrudgingly. She looked over it, then placed it in her bag.

"Okay, so what now?"

Maureen didn't answer. Instead, she grabbed her bag and walked straight out of the restaurant, not waiting for Novak. Sighing, he finished his last bite, wiped his mouth with the napkin and then, assuming it was now his responsibility, paid the bill. As he left the restaurant to catch up with Maureen, he mused to himself that his junior partner in the investigation was now very much leading the way. And here he was, obediently traipsing after her.

He followed as she continued over a few more streets, her brisk pace finally coming to a halt as she walked into a dingy-looking grocery store. By the time he had made it inside, Maureen was already at the counter, speaking to the cashier. Novak sighed and headed towards her, overhearing the end of their conversation.

"...yes, an envelope would be good."

The cashier began counting notes of cash out of the till, with Novak noticing his cheque had been placed to one side. As he stood beside Maureen, the man briefly stopped counting to observe him.

"Oh, don't worry," said Maureen calmly. "He's the one who wrote the cheque. Believe me, he should be paying me more."

The cashier smiled and continued. Once the full two thousand had been counted, the notes were placed inside a brown envelope that he slid across the counter. Maureen took hold of it but lifted the top twenty-dollar bill out carefully and passed it back to the man.

She lowered her voice and winked at him. "No rush to send the cheque. I know how slow the postal service can be."

Now he had seen the evidence of her sudden burst of inspiration, Novak fully appreciated what Maureen had done. Cheques normally took a few working days to clear, but by utilising the delays in sending it across state lines, as well as now bribing the sender, there would be no evidence of the transaction for a while yet.

As they left the grocery store, he muttered, "I do hope you'll pay me back."

"You'll just have to trust me," she replied, with a mischievous glint in her eye.

"So where now? I hope all that was in aid of something?"

Maureen pointed him in the direction of their next destination. "Yep, we have a train to catch."

They arrived at South Station's dignified exterior, its stone façade sloping and curving around the corner of the intersection like the edges of a crown, and made their way through the grand, grey station's central archway, beneath its looming clock where Maureen waited at the nearest available counter. A small woman with a warm, round face and bright red lipstick, in a ruby jacket, was waiting behind the desk.

"How can I help you, ma'am?" she asked brightly.

"Could I buy two return tickets to Chicago, please? The one that's leaving next would be perfect."

"Of course."

The woman took the cash from Maureen and carefully slotted it into her register, exchanging the payment for a set of paper tickets that slid out of the machine next to her, like sausage meat at a butcher's. Maureen thanked her and tucked them safely in her bag.

She returned to Novak, who was standing underneath a bright, giant orb in the centre of the building's ceiling. "The train for Chicago leaves in twenty minutes."

"Good. It gives me time to go and buy something for the trip."

He said no more and immediately disappeared towards the shops on the station's busy first floor. Maureen was irritated; she had always been an anxious traveller and wanted to get to their platform a good while before the train arrived, just to be sure. Her foot began to tap against the floor as she grew more and more impatient. With less than ten minutes before their scheduled departure, Novak finally returned, seemingly with nothing new in his possession.

"Please tell me you didn't just waste all that time and not even buy anything?"

He opened his jacket slightly and Maureen glimpsed a glass bottle of golden brown liquid tucked in an inside pocket.

"Seriously? You bought whisky?"

Novak smirked. "Boston to Chicago is a twenty-two-hour journey. I'm not sure I can spend that long with you completely sober. Now come on, we're going to miss our train..."

Maureen clenched her jaw and walked with him to their platform. The train had arrived so they boarded and manoeuvred their way around the other passengers to take their places in adjacent seats towards the back of the carriage. They slumped themselves down and placed their bags by their feet. Maureen felt adrenaline running through her; there was something strangely invigorating about going on the run.

As the evening gradually started to draw in, the sky darkened and the carriage took on a quieter and calmer atmosphere. The train continued to speed past fields, Maureen looked out at the mountains and rivers in the distance and her anxiety began to disperse.

Novak decided this was the moment to crack upon his bottle of bourbon. He held the bottle straight to his lips and took a hearty swig, only noticing Maureen's disapproving eyes as he lowered it back to his lap.

"What?"

"We're in the middle of a dangerous investigation and you're drinking whisky from the bottle?"

"I'm afraid this is how we did it back then. I'd venture a guess that some of this country's biggest cases have been cracked over a bottle of whisky."

He held the bottle out towards her invitingly.

"Come on. It won't hurt."

Maureen remained unmoved for a few seconds, leaving his arm awkwardly outstretched in the space between them. She was caught between her natural instinct to reject and disagree with him on everything and the feeling that she was somehow failing a test of her character. She eventually took the bottle from him and took a sip herself. The oaky sweetness was initially soothing and pleasant before the fire of the alcohol touched the back of her throat. She winced and handed the bottle back to him.

"Don't worry. It gets easier with each sip," he said, with a melancholic clarity.

And so the bottle of bourbon was passed between them as the journey continued. Maureen began to feel the alcohol take a hold of her, but mixed with her exhaustion it only made her slow down, with everything from her speech to her movements becoming more careful and relaxed. Novak's eyes too became slightly glazed.

"So, tell me," he started abruptly. "How does one come to be an acclaimed investigative journalist?"

Maureen couldn't tell if he was mocking her or not, but found that she had more and more to add to her answer as it went along. "I don't know. I guess I've always been obsessed with getting to the bottom of things. Even when I was little, I can remember the sensation of really wanting, needing even, to find something out if I didn't know it. It ate away at me, that feeling of uncertainty. And now when I hear people argue about something, say what's the longest river in the world, for example, they debate it and by the end neither of them actually know, and still believe exactly what they did before. I couldn't bear that!"

Novak nodded along politely, and Maureen noticed that his smug and superior demeanour had faded, replaced by a different expression, one that she couldn't quite decipher.

He asked another question. "And how does that work with the relationships in your life?"

"What do you mean, 'relationships'?"

"You know, the people closest to you," he said, not breaking from holding her gaze.

"What is this? *Letterman?*"

"I'm just expressing an interest," said Novak, resting his arm on the windowsill and leaning further into the chair.

Maureen paused, then decided to grace him with an answer. "I guess I have found it hard to commit to someone in the past. Maybe that's to do with my father, I don't know. I think I just know how easy it is to lose someone, in loads of different ways. So what's the point in getting over-attached? You're just setting yourself up for a fall."

Novak seemed to flash an inward smile.

"Oh, now you're judging me, are you?" said Maureen, offended. "Please by all means tell me your secrets of love; your divorce certainly would seem to make you an expert."

He took his arm off the windowsill and rested it on his lap once more, in what seemed like a defensive gesture. Maureen saw his smile fade and his eyes suddenly fill with sadness and she felt an instant pang of guilt that caused a pit in her stomach.

"I'm sorry, Novak, I shouldn't..."

"It's fine," he said. "You're right, I'm certainly not the expert, but I wasn't judging you. All I'd say is that you shouldn't be afraid of making a commitment at some point. Even if it doesn't work out, it's worth the effort to try."

Maureen fell silent and studied his face, the light of the setting sun from outside highlighting his features. There was still an innate strength and roughness to his appearance, but in their recent meetings she'd also seen a vulnerability. He didn't meet her eyes this time and instead stared out at the scenery, lost in thought, though of what she couldn't work out.

After a while, their tiredness, mixed with the guiding hand of the bourbon, caused both to drift gently into sleep. When Maureen awoke, it took her a full minute to remember where she was. The morning light was harsh on her eyes and she couldn't have guessed whether she had been asleep for one hour or ten and she looked anxiously out of the window to assess their progress. A look at her watch and the announcement of the conductor finally eased her mind. They would shortly be arriving in Buffalo.

Maureen sprang into action and gathered her things before shoving Novak's arm roughly, jolting him awake. His eyes were red and glazed with confusion as she told him to get ready to get off. He didn't question her and quickly gathered himself to follow her onto the platform. It seemed he was much more obedient after half a bottle of whisky and a few hours' sleep.

The train chugged to a stop and the two of them disembarked onto the platform. It was only then that Novak, seeing the station sign, spoke up.

"Wait! This isn't Chicago. What are you doing?"

Maureen turned to face him. "We were never really going to Chicago. If they're tracking us that's where they'll follow us to. Besides, Buffalo is closer to where we really want to go."

Still looking dazed, he stumbled down the steps beside her. Maureen continued to blink away the tiredness from her eyes as they made their way out of the station into the frosty air. She led the way to the nearest taxi.

"Where you headed, ma'am?" asked the driver.

"Niagara Falls, please?" asked Maureen, putting on an excited, girlish voice.

"Sure thing. Is it a honeymoon?" asked the driver, gesturing to Novak, who was standing blankly beside her.

"We're working on it!" said Maureen and threw her bags in the back before getting in herself. Novak sat down beside her and looked at her disapprovingly. Maureen had found the whole exchange highly entertaining and had to stop herself from giggling.

Gradually, Novak worked out Maureen's plan. They were not in fact going sightseeing but heading for the border control near the famous waterfall. They wouldn't get away with a flight out of America, but Canada was a completely different story. As he fully woke up from his slumber, Novak looked across at Maureen. She raised her eyebrows as if to ask for his thoughts. He turned away from her but allowed his chin to stoop downwards in a subtle but unmistakeable nod of approval.

Maureen instructed the driver to take them to the Canadian

side of the border and over the Rainbow Bridge. The car joined a
line of other travellers and Maureen began to feel nervous as the
border check gates and the guards standing watch beside them
came into view. All her logic dictated that whoever was on their
trail surely wouldn't have reached the Canadian border point this
quickly. It was the simplest way she could think of to leave the
country. But the uncertainty remained. She distracted herself by
looking at the scenery, watching giant spires of mist rise off the
surface of the water that glinted in the light of the rising sun, as it
came crashing down the falls in the distance.

Finally, the taxi made a slow approach up the narrow corridor
between the bollards and they pulled up to the kiosk. Her nerves
weren't helped by the appearance of the guard in the small
window to their left, a rough and wiry-faced man with a snarl like
an angry bulldog.

"Documentation, please," he snapped.

She handed their passports through the window and he
opened each of them carefully and flicked through the pages, his
eyes combing over every detail. An almost unbearable tension fell
over the taxi. The man finally made a grunt of approval and
returned the passports to them, directing the driver to the next
point. Maureen closed the window and breathed a quiet sigh of
relief.

They instructed the driver to stop once they had cleared the
hangover of traffic from the crossing and navigated to the nearest
bus station, a modest building with a flat, low roof tucked into a
lay-by off one of the main roads into St Catharines. Maureen
thanked and paid him, flashing a sweet smile as he wished them
all the best. They bought tickets for the next bus to Toronto
airport and waited in the lounge, a square room with pale wooden
benches symmetrically placed on each side, whose purple carpet
bore the stains of hundreds of previous journeys. There was a
dusty television set suspended in the far corner, showing pictures
of an American news channel on mute.

It was only now that Novak engaged Maureen in conversation properly for the first time since they'd left the train.

"You can be quite smart sometimes, you know."

"I take it you're happy with the plan then?"

"I've seen worse," he grumbled, to her quiet delight.

Suddenly, the picture on the television caught Maureen's attention. It took her brain a couple of seconds to process what was familiar to her about the images. There was a photograph next to the newscaster reporting on the story. The face belonged to a man she had last seen tied to his own living-room chair, the smug, tanned face of Don Cassidy.

Maureen rose to her feet and walked closer to the television, not taking her eyes off it. Her heart sunk and she felt the fear snaking throughout her body. She intently studied the text that ran alongside the report.

Leading FBI Agent found dead in home in Washington. Investigation ongoing.

It froze her to the spot. It didn't make sense. She had last seen Cassidy barely twenty-four hours earlier and now he was dead. Novak slowly trudged to stand beside her, his lack of communication seemingly confirming that he too had seen the report. Maureen felt herself go numb, as if all the blood had been drained out of her. Once the shock slowly began to dissipate, she couldn't decide what emotion had replaced it. It was somewhere between fear and guilt.

Novak spoke, breaking her from her trance. "I'm guessing you had nothing to do with this?"

"No," Maureen spluttered, realising her mouth had gone dry. "I don't understand..."

"I'm sure it wasn't your fault," he said, clearly knowing exactly what she was thinking.

The photograph disappeared from the screen and the

newscaster moved on to another story. That was all the information they were going to get. The two of them stood in silence, struck by the realisation that the stakes of their investigation were getting higher and higher.

Maureen thought through the possibilities. Had Cassidy been punished for the information leak? Or had he done the job himself before anyone had had the chance? She rushed to the door of the station and flung it open before hunching over in the corner of a pebbled patio and vomiting. The sensation had come out of nowhere and she'd had no more than a couple of seconds to react. She rested her hand against the cold wall to support herself. A palm was placed gently on her back and she became aware of Novak's presence.

"Are you okay?" he asked.

"Yeah," she muttered.

"The bus will be here in a minute."

"Okay. I'll be fine, just give me a moment." She staggered back to her feet.

The bus pulled into the station and they were soon at the airport, with its strange and ornate glass roof that seemed to protrude into the building, showering it with the sunlight from the outside. The pair hurried to the nearest departures board and scanned the rows for the next available flight to Kiev. After a few moments, Maureen excitedly tapped Novak on the arm; there was one later that day. The Polish airline's desk was not far away but as they approached Novak held Maureen back before they reached the velvet rope.

"What?" she asked.

"I don't think we have enough cash left to cover the flights."

He was right. They were going to have to come up with some more money somehow, risk their cards being tracked or find another way to fund the flight. Novak scratched his chin and Maureen mentally took herself into the contents of her own purse. And then an idea came to her, and she delved inside it to produce a bright red card.

Novak glanced at it dismissively. "They'll track credit cards too."

"It's not mine," said Maureen mischievously.

"What?"

"It's my mother's. She gave it to me when I was young, 'for emergencies'. Let's just say I ended up having quite a few 'emergencies' in my teens!"

Novak looked appalled. "Won't she mind?"

Maureen shook her head. "Don't worry, Boy Scout, I'll pay her back. Now do you want to go to Kiev or not?" With that, she sauntered up to the desk.

A gradual realisation appeared on Novak's face. "Hang on, if you had this the whole time, then why did I have to pay you two grand?"

"That was still a far safer method. They could be tracking my mum's card too. Except now, we'll already be on a plane by the time they see it come through."

She left him to walk purposefully up to the front desk and he muttered under his breath. "Unbelievable..."

A few hours later, the two of them boarded the final leg of their great escape. Maureen stared out of the window at the tarmac, still aware of the adrenaline surging around her system. Thoughts of Cassidy had stayed with her, but she tried to ignore them. There was nothing they could do about that now; it was going to have to wait until they returned. Allowing her eyes to close, Maureen waited patiently for the plane to take off so that she could use the soothing hum of the jets to return to some much-needed sleep.

CHAPTER FOURTEEN

The Boston office that the FBI were using for the investigation was a small, pokey room, with windows that faced out onto the busy streets below and one long table that covered nearly the entirety of the room. It reminded Rick Nelson of the room in *12 Angry Men*, though thankfully without the heat. Nelson was the leading officer on the Finn–Novak case and had travelled to Boston specifically to oversee the surveillance that had been placed on the pair of them.

He had been an athlete in his teenage years and had maintained his muscular build, while his hair had been perfectly placed in a thin line of fringe a few inches above his eyes. He had inherited a strong, deep voice from his father and that, combined with his height and stature, helped him to appear more senior than his age would suggest. Nelson was determined to prove himself to his superiors in the Bureau by handling the case as efficiently as he could, ignoring its peculiar nature.

He arrived at the office in the morning with a cup of coffee in hand and took off his jacket before hanging it on the back of the chair at the head of the long table. Then he placed the coffee down and rolled up his sleeves. This was a ritual of his, as if he was physically signalling to the others in the room that it was time to get to work.

The agents who had been charged with bugging Maureen Finn's apartment and recording her movements were named Lukas and Totty. Lukas was earnest and eager to please, which fitted his straight-out-of-college appearance, while Totty was older, fatter and more relaxed. They were waiting in the office as Nelson arrived.

"All right, gentlemen. What's the latest?"

"Not a lot to report really, sir. The girl has stayed in her apartment all weekend and is due to visit her mother tonight."

"What, she didn't go out at all?" asked Nelson.

"Not as far as we know."

He looked sceptical but pushed past it. "And what about Novak in New York?"

Lukas and Totty shared a slightly nervous look and neither rushed to speak.

Eventually, Lukas muttered, "We still haven't found any trace of him since the incident at his apartment when our agents were apprehended."

Nelson looked out of the window. That had been a slip-up. Being arrested by local police was never going to look particularly good. But it had just been a clever move by Novak. This wasn't their average person of interest, but an ex-intelligence man who knew the tricks of the trade.

"He's smart, that Novak," said Totty, with a hint of admiration that annoyed Nelson.

"If anything she's the smart one," he replied. "But we can't afford to underestimate them any longer. I'm certain Novak will have gone to warn Finn of our surveillance. You're sure there's been no sighting of him in Boston?"

"Not as far as we know," said Lukas again, meekly.

"Keep looking into it. And you're absolutely certain she hasn't left her apartment this weekend?"

"As I said, the only conversation we heard was her arranging tonight's dinner with her mother. She was probably resting after she got back from Washington."

Nelson was getting more agitated and began to rant aimlessly at the room. "She's not a goddamn mute though, is she?! You're telling me that our equipment picked up no other sound across the whole weekend?"

Lukas started to go red in the face and looked at Totty for some kind of approval as whether to mention anything else. Totty looked blank.

"Well..." Lukas started. "She did listen to some opera."

"Opera?" Nelson barked.

"Yes. 'The Coronation of Poppea', I believe."

"I don't think that's relevant..." started Totty, but Nelson hushed him with an outstretched hand.

"Wait. How loud was it? Loud enough so you couldn't hear anything else?" asked Nelson, his mind ticking into action.

"Yes, sir," said Lukas.

"Novak was there," Nelson said sternly. "He told her about the bugs and she used the opera to cover their conversation. They're up to something. Get me footage of every bus or train station in the city. Any possible route out of here, I want to see camera footage for."

Neither Lukas nor Totty moved at first. It was only when he fixed them with a cold, steely look that they burst into action. Both hurriedly jumped to their feet and rushed past him out of the office. Nelson leant forwards on the back of a chair and continued to stare absently out into the city. He had a feeling that something was off. Novak and Finn were headed somewhere, but where?

The answer was revealed to him later that afternoon. Lukas enthusiastically returned to the office, nearly taking the door off its hinges as he burst back into the room.

"We've got an image of them in South Station on Saturday, sir."

Nelson rose from the chair and fired questions back at his agent.

"I knew it. Right, anything on their credit card statements? Any purchases of tickets? We need the destination as soon as possible."

"Nothing yet, sir. Is it possible they paid in cash?"

Nelson mused on this for a second, before deciding that that was almost certainly what they had done. He walked purposefully straight past Lukas, muttering as he exited the office: "I'm going down there. I'm not losing them."

He caught a taxi straight to the station and marched into the building, immediately heading to the service desk. There were five or so people waiting in a queue but he cut straight to the front of the line, generating a few protests from the bemused Bostonians behind him before he stuck out his FBI badge without even looking in their direction, and the complaints disappeared. There was a meek-looking, bald man behind the counter and he seemed to melt into his chair as Nelson faced him up.

"Agent Nelson, FBI. I'm looking for a suspect who was pictured leaving this station on Saturday. I need to speak to anyone who was working on the ticket desk that day."

"Yes... of course. Yes, uh, one second, please."

The man slid back on his chair so he was out of sight of the square window and after a few moments another man's head appeared, looming over the first. He beckoned Nelson forward.

"If you'd like to come round the back, sir, I will locate any colleagues who were working on Saturday."

Nelson was led through a private door that led into a beige break room, with old, tattered sofas and coffee tables covered with half-drunk mugs of cold, curdling coffee. There were a few staff members there and all of them looked at him with a mixture of fear and excitement. It was a look Nelson had seen before and one he had come to enjoy.

The manager who had invited him in gestured towards a chair and then disappeared. One by one, a series of men and women in ruby jackets arrived and cautiously took seats around the room. Nelson made sure to fix each with a stern expression of suspicion. Making them uncomfortable would hopefully speed the process up. And he was already running out of time.

Finally, the manager told him everyone was present and Nelson cleared his throat and got to his feet, walking into the open space in the middle of the break room where he was visible to all.

"Okay. Now there is no need for concern from any of you. I am simply looking for your assistance in an incredibly important operation that we are running. We are looking for two suspects. One is a white man, mid-fifties, similar height and build to myself. Name is Robert Novak. The other is a woman, early thirties, relatively tall for a lady, brown hair. Name of Maureen Finn. Now I realise you will all have seen hundreds of passengers on Saturday but I want you to think carefully if those descriptions bring back any memories. And I would add that if anyone you saw was acting suspiciously, then it is worth telling me. Perhaps they seemed in a particular rush to leave. I'm afraid the only other information I can give you is that they likely paid in cash."

He paused and put his hands on his hips, waiting for the first voice to break through the silence in the room. His eyes scanned the station employees constantly, but few would hold his gaze. The silence continued. A few at least made the effort to look like they were thinking about it. Others looked blank and frightened. He was just about to speak again, to encourage them, when a gentle voice was heard from the corner of the room.

"I served a woman that sounds like your description, sir."

Nelson pivoted on his heel to look at where it had come from. There was a small woman with a round face, her lips accentuated by bright red lipstick. She had her hand raised in the air, like a shy child at the back of a classroom.

"Yes, thank you, Miss. Can you tell me anything you remember about your encounter?"

The woman spoke slowly. "I recall that she wanted to catch the next train available. And she paid in cash, despite the fact it was a large fare."

Novak's heart rate rose and he found himself striding closer to her. "Where was she going?"

The woman swallowed and then stared up at him sheepishly. "She bought two return tickets to Chicago, sir."

Nelson immediately sent out a radio message to all of the agents working on the case to contact the Chicago headquarters and look for footage of the station. He returned to the office and found himself unable to sit still for the rest of the day, constantly changing position and drumming his fingers impatiently on the table. A couple of hours passed with no news, and even after he had spoken to an old colleague who worked in Chicago himself there was still no evidence of Novak and Finn arriving in the Second City.

Losing hope, he barked at Lukas to go and find a map; needing a visual representation of their journey, both to work out where they may have headed and, just as importantly, what their overall intention was. Lukas returned with a poster-sized map of the country that he had brought from a souvenir shop and he unfurled it onto the table as Totty moved documents out of the way. Nelson came and stood over it, eyes fixed on the contents.

Lukas took out a pencil and ruler and began to draw a line across the map, starting at Boston. "This is the route they took to get to Chicago and all the locations the train passes on its way."

Nelson followed the pencil line as he drew, the route leaving Massachusetts and then going through New York State, briefly skating along the edges of Vermont before it followed the curve of the border down and finally through Ohio and Indiana before stopping in Illinois.

"Where else might they have got off the train?" asked Totty.

"It's nearly a thousand-mile stretch. There are so many places they could have been aiming for," added Lukas in a defeated tone.

Nelson ignored them and continued to fixate on the line drawn on the map. His mind played every scenario he could think of as his eyes passed through each destination. Suddenly, he stopped at the point where the line veered into Buffalo. His gaze rose to look at the name of the city in the space above it, written in bold. Toronto.

"They got off here," said Nelson, thrusting the tip of his finger onto the map.

"Why?" asked Lukas, looking at where Nelson was indicating.

"They weren't trying to cross the country, they were trying to get out of it," he said, dragging his finger upwards to illustrate his point. "Through Canada."

Nelson stood back triumphantly and allowed his agents to catch up with him. Then he raised his voice and belted out an instruction like a military order.

"Right. I want to know the details of every single flight that left Toronto airport yesterday. I don't care if it was going to Timbuktu, I want everything. And I want to speak to somebody at the airport immediately." He looked at Lukas and Totty with his forehead tensed forwards. "Call your wives, boys. You're not getting home anytime soon."

CHAPTER FIFTEEN

Around an hour or so after their plane landed in Kiev, Maureen and Novak arrived at the Grand Duke Hotel. They weren't spoilt for choice with accommodation in the city and Maureen had simply instructed the driver of the taxi to take them to the nearest hotel. The Grand Duke couldn't have been the nearest, but she sensed that the man had wanted to show them one of the nicer buildings Kiev had to offer, or perhaps he just wanted a backhander for bringing them new custom.

Maureen hadn't known what to expect of this mysterious eastern metropolis. A place that lagged behind its western counterparts by a century or so, or a futuristic, robotic industrial labyrinth. As the taxi pulled away from the airport and towards the busier centre, she noticed the rows and rows of large, dreary grey buildings, with the occasional flash of more ambitious or colourful architecture in between. The sky was cloudless and stark and the sidewalks were large and clean. There were plenty of cars parked alongside the roads, though noticeably fewer than in Boston, and webs of telephone wires that passed above them, between roofs and ducking around the branches of bare and sinuous trees.

And then, in the distance, the daunting figure of a giant woman, fashioned in steel. A magnificently powerful image, with her sword and shield held high, pointing towards the sky. It pleased Maureen to witness such a titanic vision of feminine strength and her eyes continued to stray back in the statue's direction, even as they neared their stop.

The hotel was large and Gothic in appearance, with rows of windows stretching upwards in perfectly straight lines across its front. The doors were opened for them as they approached. The interior of the building was bright and decadent, marble and gold illuminated with amber lighting. Maureen and Novak shared a glance as they took it in, but the thing they found most welcome was a reprieve from the biting chill of the wind outside.

They walked over to the reception desk. A man with wafer-thin grey hair and spectacles balanced on the bridge of his oversized nose greeted them. "Welcome to the Grand Duke," he said in perfect English, though with a thick accent. "I take it you would like a room? We have some very romantic options, perfect for couples like yourselves."

Maureen smiled and looked at Novak. This time, he also smirked.

"I think two rooms would be better," said Maureen and the man bowed his head in a mixture of embarrassment and perhaps even slight disappointment.

They paid for their rooms, having converted their leftover cash into karbovanets, and took the keys from the man behind the desk, before being directed to the elevator in the corner of the lobby. Once inside, Novak's serious tone returned.

"Okay. So we're here. Now what's the plan?"

"You're the ex-FBI man. Don't you have any contacts we could use?"

"None that wouldn't immediately reveal our whereabouts."

"And I can't imagine we want to go asking too many questions here about ex-KGB officers. Not this soon after independence."

"There must be another way to find Tambov, surely?"

A memory rushed to the front of Maureen's mind. "Chess!" she exclaimed. "He was a world-leading chess player. The FBI files said so. There must be some kind of records on chess players."

Novak nodded. "I'll talk to the concierge. They'll be able to point us in the right direction."

"Meet you back at the lobby in half an hour," said Maureen, as the elevator juddered to a halt.

When they reconvened, Novak already had a destination in mind. He had spoken to the concierge about chess playing in the city and the man had informed him that Kiev residents would gather in Shevchenko Park to play against each other on the boards there. Maureen was enthused by the news. A keen player like Tambov would surely have visited the spot at some point.

Shevchenko Park was a square green space in the centre of the city, near the university. It was named after the literary figure Taras Shevchenko, and a statue of him stood at the park's midpoint with a circular path surrounding it and rows of red flowers blossoming in bushes on its perimeter. To the left of the statue was an area of concrete, with odd booths dotted around, composed of parallel stone benches with small tables in the middle. Each table bore the markings of a traditional chessboard and many were filled by people of all generations playing the game.

Maureen and Novak sat down at one of the booths and watched the other players carefully, looking for anyone who resembled the images of Tambov they had seen in the FBI folder of Sean Finn. Maureen scanned the faces of those around them, but none seemed to fit the description. Tambov didn't appear to be present. They were going to have to try something else.

She turned to Novak and found his eyes fixed on a player a few paces to their right. A man with a long beard made up of patches of black and grey, wearing a dark, ragged overcoat. He was chatting away enthusiastically in a language she couldn't understand. Every time he moved a piece on the board, he followed it with a minute or two of exuberant gesture and discussion, his eyes wild with excitement.

"What is it? Why are you watching him?" Maureen asked.

Novak didn't break his gaze, but muttered, "The language he's speaking. It's not Ukrainian. It's Russian."

They waited for the man to finish his game. Eventually, he achieved checkmate and the figure seated across from him rose from the bench and walked away. The man who had been speaking Russian began carefully gathering the pieces and reordering them on the board. As he did so, Maureen slid herself shyly onto the vacant bench. The man lifted his head to look at her.

"Excuse me. Do you speak English?" Maureen asked.

The man scoffed. "Of course," he said gruffly. "And I don't suppose you speak Russian, do you, American girl?"

Maureen ignored the jibe. "I'm afraid not. I apologise for interrupting you, but I was admiring your passion for the game."

"Chess is more than a game. It is an art. It defies time and borders," said the man.

"I agree," said Maureen. "In fact, my colleague and I are writing a book on the great chess players. My name is Maureen Finn. Do you mind if I sit with you for a while?"

The man sized her up, but she could tell she had softened him with her false affection for his beloved game. After a moment, he nodded. "My name is Piotr Eristoff."

"Thank you, Mr Eristoff," said Maureen. Novak stayed silent, lurking behind her on the bench, watching Eristoff closely. "Why don't you tell us about your experience of this 'art' that you love so much?"

Eristoff didn't need much persuading. "Of course, you see my country produces the finest players in the world. This is because of our academies. We treat chess like you Americans treat your reading and mathematics."

"Fascinating," said Maureen, resting her head on her palm to exaggerate her interest in Eristoff's words. "And why do you think that is?"

"My country used chess to show the world that we are not the uneducated savages who live in the cold like they think we are, but that we are great thinkers, planners and strategists."

Maureen noticed it was the second time he had used the words "my country", and he had followed each utterance with a nervous glance around him. She guessed that mentioning the Soviet Union by name was a risky game in Kiev at the moment.

She attempted to steer the conversation closer to the information she was after. "I agree that chess is very transferrable, do you think it has helped its players in other areas? Some say that planning for a war is just one large game of chess."

Eristoff paused for a moment. "Perhaps, but first let me tell you a little more about the history. To fully understand something you must go back to the start, you understand?"

Novak sighed and rolled his eyes but Maureen ignored him. "I do. Please go on, Mr Eristoff."

"Chess was introduced to Russia more than one thousand years ago, by traders who came from the Middle East. Tsar Ivan the Fourth – Ivan the Terrible – died while playing chess! These are the details you need to record in your book. You must respect chess for what it is."

"Indeed, Mr Eristoff. One of my favourite stories is about the great Mikhail Chigorin..."

"Yes?" said Eristoff, leaning forwards in evident interest.

"Apparently, when Chigorin travelled internationally, friends would ask him how he managed to speak to people of different languages. He said, 'I don't have to. I speak the international language of chess.'"

Eristoff smiled warmly for the first time and rocked on his bench. "So true, so true," he mumbled to himself.

Now she had proven her interest, she tried a more direct question.

"Do you know Victor Tambov? I heard he lives in Kiev now."

"Of course I know Victor. I play with him once a week. I never win, of course," said Eristoff.

Maureen felt excitement rush through her and struggled to keep her questions calm. "Mr Tambov must have a lot to tell us about his experiences. Do you know where we might be able to speak to him?"

"No," said Eristoff, and Maureen's shoulders sank. "He's a very private man, Victor. I only meet him by chance here in the park, or sometimes we arrange to meet at a café in Pechersk Lavra."

Maureen seized on this new lead. "Could you tell us anything about this café? Anything you can offer us, Mr Eristoff. I just want to be able to talk with one of the great players. I can't leave Kiev knowing I didn't try."

Eristoff nodded his head. "It faces the bell tower. If the sun is out, then you should sit in the tower's shadow. That's all I can tell you."

Maureen noticed that the man's initial rudeness had melted away with the discussion of his beloved game and now he appeared warm and cordial. Maureen began to wonder if he was a grandfather. She had softened to the eccentric old man.

"Thank you so much for your help, Mr Eristoff. I will be sure to mention you in my book."

His face lit up as he bade them goodbye. Maureen turned to look at Novak, expecting a positive comment.

"Brilliant. So now we have to wait by some random tower for a man we're not sure will ever turn up."

"It's something at least. We need to try."

"I wasn't expecting much else from an old loony sitting in a park."

"I liked him. He was a character."

"How the hell did you know that thing about Chigorin?"

Maureen gave him a patronising stare that he was becoming more and more familiar with. "I didn't. I made it up."

CHAPTER SIXTEEN

Pechersk Lavra was an entirely different part of Kiev and by far its most unique and impressive. The district was founded on the site of an old monastery and Maureen had heard that it had recently been granted UNESCO World Heritage status. It was located on the other side of the city to Shevchenko Park, with its fringes overlooking the cold, grey waters of the Dnipro River.

When Maureen and Novak first caught a glimpse of the area and its various buildings, they both took a moment to briefly forget their mission and take in one of the world's most impressive architectural wonders. The dull, concrete towers of the city, dripping in communist practicality, disappeared from view and were instead replaced by ivory white, castle-like buildings that stretched across the hillside, interspersed with bushy trees. The central, baroque churches were capped with grassy green tiles, which then led up to magnificent spires of gold. Every building seemed perfectly positioned with the next, which gave the whole district the feel of a great, expansive courtyard.

Next to the church stood the tallest of the buildings, towering above the rest of Pechersk Lavra. This was the famous bell tower

Eristoff had spoken of. It continued the colour scheme of white, green and gold, but it had a tiered structure, with the stages growing smaller the further up the tower they stretched, which gave it the appearance of a narrow and delicate wedding cake. One that could only be served at the most stylish and expensive wedding.

They walked slowly over the cobbled streets that lined the monastery, taking in as much of their surroundings as they could. The streets weren't busy, with only the odd passer-by ever in view. As they got closer to the base of the tower, Novak pointed ahead and Maureen saw that, even through the cover of a smattering of clouds, there was enough sun for a period of shade on the ground shielded behind the bell tower. As they continued, they noticed a collection of plain folding chairs gathered around a kiosk on the corner. Maureen strode over and took a seat, feeling motivated. They had found the café that Eristoff had described. Now it was a question of whether or not Tambov would put in an appearance.

Novak bought coffee from the kiosk and came to sit with her, the two of them facing back towards the tower, necks slightly craned to admire its soaring beauty.

"Nice spot, isn't it?" he said.

"It's wonderful," said Maureen and they shared a smile, though half hidden by the cups of coffee they held to their lips.

She dipped a hand into her bag and withdrew the photograph from her father's FBI file, the one with the image of Tambov, those manic, bright eyes staring back at the camera. Maureen laid it on the table so Novak could remind himself of the man they were looking for. She began to pointedly stare at the faces of nearby people, both those already seated at the café and those simply passing it.

Novak noticed her and interrupted her train of thought. "Maureen... you do realise this is a long shot. At best."

Maureen looked back at him irritably. "I know, but we've come this far, haven't we?"

Novak sat back and continued watching her distracted and ever-changing gaze. A thought popped into his mind. He recognised something within her. That unflinching determination, bordering on obsession, to finish a case. He realised that this mission was starting to overcome her and he found himself feelings pangs of guilt at being the one to have brought this curse upon her. A curse that he understood better than most.

Maureen noticed the strange look on his face. "What?"

He shook his head and brushed the thought away. "Nothing."

As expected, hours passed with no sign of Tambov. They ordered more coffees to keep their energy up and their hands warm. Novak realised that Maureen was prepared to wait until dark at least, and that any words of reservation would only be met with anger. So, instead, he sat quietly, tapping his foot under the table. To try and fill the time, he brought up a topic he hadn't managed to update Maureen on yet.

"I managed to do some digging on Dirk Hauptman."

"Oh yeah?" said Maureen, only half-listening.

"It was an interesting case. He was a union leader, a big-hitter back in his day, who committed suicide after he was accused of being a communist."

This prompted a reaction from Maureen, turning to focus on him directly. "Oh God, that's awful. The damned Red Scare!" She paused and added, more sternly, "Why would that have anything to do with my father though?"

"He was the person put in charge of investigating him. And I think Kennedy was the one who ordered him to do it."

"What makes you say that?"

"To secure the support of the unions in the election."

"You really think Kennedy was capable of something so underhand?"

Novak snorted. "What man gets to that position of power without having to go over to the dark side once in a while?"

Maureen let this new information digest in her mind. It was certainly important. She had heard about the role the unions played in previous elections. Had Kennedy told her father to target an innocent man? In order to gain power? And then new questions emerged, more pertinent to their investigation: Was that the moment her father had lost faith in his former friend? Was that the starting pistol that had ultimately led to the meetings with Oswald and Tambov and finally to the president's death?

Novak waited silently for her to respond and eventually she mustered a retort. "It's starting to come together, but there's still too many missing pieces."

He nodded and she returned to a position facing out into the street, observing all the people who passed under the tower. Novak looked at the buildings around them, in a more ruminative manner.

"It's funny. I didn't imagine Kiev to be like this at all," he said.

"What do you mean?"

"I guess you get a picture in your mind of what you imagine the Eastern Bloc to be like. A cold, bleak place. I guess the government tried their best to create that. To paint America as some kind of Utopia, the land of the free. Where the sun always shines. And the Soviet Union as dark and empty."

"Things are rarely as simple as that. Especially when it's our government telling us they are," said Maureen, with a wry smile.

"This little scene could be part of a much more glamorous city," said Novak. "Florence, Vienna. Paris even."

"You've been to Paris?" said Maureen, with obvious condescension.

"Why is anything I do that is remotely cultural such a surprise to you?"

Maureen giggled. "It just doesn't suit you, I suppose."

"Thanks very much," said Novak. "I've actually been to Paris twice, I'll have you know. Once for work and again... with my wife."

The pain returned to his face, which Maureen recognised from their exchanges by the esplanade and on the train to Buffalo. She found herself wanting to reach out to him, to finally ask the question she had so far avoided. Instead, the sight of a man quietly taking a seat at table three to the right of them caught her eye. The man wore a plain overcoat and had wild, grey hair, with circular glasses on the bridge of his nose. Maureen found herself looking closer at him. He had the look of a musician or artist, an air of stylishness and eccentricity that marked him out from the other people around him, as well as a poise and innate dignity that seemed more fitting of an older, forgotten period. Maureen peered at the glasses and realised that the pair of eyes they were shielding had become a fixture in her head over the previous few hours.

"That's him," she said, bashing her palm down on Novak's arm. "That's Tambov. It must be."

Novak turned slowly, making sure to look upwards at the buildings before slowly dropping his gaze towards the man. He didn't seem to notice their attention so Novak inspected him, before returning to the picture on the table. The man was older and frailer than his photographed counterpart, but there was something inherent that they shared. He agreed with Maureen. This had to be the man they were looking for.

"Okay, let's go over. And let me do the talking," he said, worried her excitement would scare the man away. He wasn't going to blow the opportunity they'd been given.

The two of them slowly approached the table. The man's attention was fixed on the bell tower that loomed behind them, which he looked upon with an expression of knowing admiration.

Novak said his name aloud. "Victor Tambov?"

The man snapped into an immediate state of alertness, his

bright blue eyes locking onto them, flashing with the same intensity that they recognised from the photos.

He answered in Russian: "Yes?"

Novak took a deep breath and then spoke in clunky but understandable Russian in return. "We'd like to speak to you if you wouldn't mind. We are writing a book on the great chess players."

Tambov sized him up and then leant closer to them, this time responding in perfect English. "You're from America, I see. Interesting. Long way for you to travel, just to talk about chess of all things... Where in America are you from?"

"New York," replied Novak, to barely a flicker of recognition.

Tambov's attention fell upon Maureen, who was half hidden by Novak's shoulder.

"Boston."

This seemed to mean something to Tambov. His wild eyes twinkled and he homed in on Maureen, like a falcon circling its prey.

"Boston?"

"Yes," said Maureen nervously. "Do you know it?"

"I've only been once," said Tambov, still inspecting Maureen closely. "How old are you, Miss, if you don't mind me asking such a rude and direct question?"

Maureen glanced quickly at Novak, who shrugged. "I've just turned thirty."

Suddenly, Tambov's face filled with delight, twitching violently as if he had just received a sharp shot of adrenaline directly into his bloodstream. "Sean. Sean Finn. You cannot be his daughter, his little... Maureen?"

Maureen swallowed the saliva that had formed in the back of her throat. She felt distinctly unnerved by this stranger from across the world recognising her so easily. Not that he seemed hostile towards her; quite the opposite. She was debating whether or not that was a good thing, whether the fact that Tambov knew her father so intimately would further clear away the fog that had for so long surrounded her perception of him or further shatter the fragile image that remained.

Tambov made a point of pulling out the two nearest chairs. "Please sit, both of you, sit."

As Novak attempted to resume the questioning, Tambov continued to stare affectionately at Maureen.

"So, Mr Tambov. Now that you know us better than we expected, I wonder if we could learn a bit more about you?"

"You really want to know about my chess career?" said Tambov suspiciously.

"Yes," continued Novak. "You said that you had been to Boston before; was that for a tournament?"

Tambov began to laugh, sitting back in his chair and allowing the hearty sounds of laughter to start in his chest and then project loudly out of his mouth. He continued for some time, finally bringing the volume down as he took off his glasses and wiped them with a handkerchief.

It was only then that he chose to answer. "Do you know why I like coming here? To Pechersk Lavra? To the great bell tower? It is because it is a place that has two sides, two separate identities. One is the beautiful, cultural front that you see before you now, the opulence of the church, the beauty of the architecture. But below our very feet is its other side. A whole other place hidden below. You see, the ancient monks who lived here created a labyrinth of underground caves and you can still access them today, yet on first visiting you would have no idea that they existed at all."

This monologue was followed by confused silence as Maureen and Novak looked at each other, unable to logically connect the answer to the question or find a way to follow up with another.

Finally, Maureen asked, "I'm sorry, Mr Tambov. What has that got to do with chess?"

Tambov sighed and began his explanation. "Well, Maureen.

May I call you Maureen? I'm making a comparison. You see, just as Pechersk Lavra appears to be a wonderful, historic monastery, it is in fact hiding a network of caves. Just like yourself and Mister Novak. You appear to be interested in my chess career, but I suspect you are in fact after something else entirely."

He sat back, evidently pleased with himself. There was no longer any point in shielding their intentions with this strange but sharp man.

"We want to talk about my father. We believe that you and he were close."

Tambov laughed once more. "We were enemies! On opposite sides of a war. I wouldn't call that close."

"And yet you recognised me, his daughter from thirty years ago, immediately?" said Maureen, raising her eyebrows.

Tambov smiled back at her. "You are certainly his daughter, that's for sure." He leant in once more, lowering his voice slightly. "If you really want to talk properly, we cannot do it here. The war may be over, but the wounds... will still take time to heal. We can go back to my house, it is not far."

Maureen looked at Novak, communicating her uncertainty with her eyes. He got the message. It was one thing talking to Tambov in the open, but quite another to go back to his home. He had at no point seemed like he had sinister intentions, but Novak was wary that they were still dealing with a man who had been at the forefront of cold war espionage. However, it was either accept the invitation or leave Kiev without the truth.

"That's kind of you, lead the way," he said decisively.

They left Pechersk Lavra and its bell tower behind, following Tambov back towards the centre of the city. The walk was carried out in near-silence with the occasional interlude where Tambov would point out a landmark and talk them through its historical significance, taking on the role of an erudite tour guide, complete with bumbling mannerisms. Maureen tuned in and out, still reeling from Tambov recognising her so quickly.

"The legend goes that Kiev was founded by three Slavic brothers. And its history after that was of constant conflict; it was a toy passed between different empires: The Mongols, the Byzantine Empire, the Polish, and of course most latterly... my country. The Nazis basically burned it to the ground, and of course they rid it entirely of its Jewish influence, and we had to build it back up. It's a city whose streets are built on bloodshed, you see. Underneath the surface, the Dnipro runs red," he said with severity, as if he was a professor hammering home the key point of his lecture.

He hadn't lied; his house was not far. They turned onto a quiet cul-de-sac with rows of terraced stone houses in parallel lines on either side, marked in front by rows of black railings mounted with small, arrow-like spikes. Tambov's house was in the middle of the terrace, marked by a large navy door. He held it open to welcome them inside.

"Please come in. The sitting room is just through there to the left."

The interior was well kept and stylish, with high ceilings and freshly painted walls. It was dim in the hallway, but as they entered the room Tambov had pointed them to, the light from the large windows illuminated the setting and allowed them to see clearer. One wall was covered entirely by two identical oak bookshelves, stretching high up towards the lofty ceiling, each shelf filled and most overflowing. Maureen saw that the majority were in Russian but recognised a few well-known English texts in the mix: Dickens, the Brontës. She even noticed a copy of Orwell's *Animal Farm*, which made her look twice. This was not what she had imagined the home of a former Soviet agent to be like.

There was a grand piano in the corner, with a view through one of the windows that overlooked a small but pleasant patch of lawn. Medals and trophies lined the mantelpiece and there was a chaise longue at an angle in the centre of the room, positioned to face a red armchair by the other window. This was where Tambov took a seat.

Maureen sat down on the chaise longue, where Novak joined her, and looked at Tambov, who was staring back at them with an expectant, almost mischievous grin.

"You may now speak as freely as you please," said Tambov.

Maureen didn't need a second invitation. "Thank you. So where did you first meet my father, Mr Tambov?"

"Berlin. At some point during the fifties. I can't remember exactly the year, I'm afraid. That was a period when time seemed to move too quickly to keep up with."

"That's all right. And how did you manage to meet an agent working on the other side?"

Tambov smiled and leant forwards to rest his elbows on his knees. "As impossible as it may seem, your father and myself had a lot in common. In fact, had we both been born in the same country, Maureen, I am certain that Sean and I would have been wonderful friends. Unfortunately, our destiny was to face each other on opposite sides of a war. And we both wanted to win, of course. However, what your father and I both understood is that there was no point in winning at all costs. I managed to get a message to him. An offer to exchange prisoners. You see, we were both losing good agents for no other reason than ego and spite. It was senseless."

"So, you started exchanging prisoners in secret?"

"It saved many lives. And it helped to ease the tension politically."

"What was your goal?"

Tambov stopped smiling and his forehead tensed up. "To ensure the cold war stayed... cold."

"And after my father had left the service, did you keep in touch?"

Now the smile returned. "Maureen. Why are you asking me

questions you already know the answers to? I had hoped we had moved past that."

Maureen corrected herself. "We know you met him in New York." She took a deep breath before adding, "Before the assassination of President Kennedy."

Tambov began to chuckle again and looked absently out of the window. "Ah. There we are. The reason for your visit to Kiev is finally revealed."

Maureen found that she was growing more incensed and ignored him. "When you met with my father, did you help him in arranging the assassination? Was it your idea to get him involved?"

"Maureen, I didn't reach out to Sean. Sean contacted me."

The revelation stung Maureen. She fidgeted and tried to settle herself by placing her hands in her lap, but she was aware that her heart was thumping. Novak took the opportunity to step in and carry on the conversation.

"What information did you give him?"

"It was a catch-up between two old friends. I was on my way out at that point, I knew that the war was fruitless. That it had no end. So I shared the information I had collected."

"You mean the government documents that you stole," said Novak, with a snarl.

"I am not a criminal, Mr Novak. You forget that wars have two sides. And I would hope you wouldn't be so foolish as to assume that you were always on the noble one."

He and Novak stared at each other, their eyes burrowing into one another's skulls.

"Did you tell him about Oswald?" interjected Maureen, unable to restrain herself.

Tambov looked at her stoically. "I did."

"Why?"

"Maureen, again you already know..."

"Say it!" said Maureen, the words coming out in an unrestrained yelp. "I don't care, I want you to say it out loud."

Tambov sighed but did as she asked. "Sean was looking for someone to do the job. Someone connected to the Soviet Union, but not too closely. Someone with a hatred of America, who wouldn't take any convincing. Someone who could be manipulated easily. And Oswald fitted the bill."

Silence filled the room. Maureen felt herself go numb, as if a cold wind had just brushed over her. She found herself unable to speak and it took her a few moments to even look up in Novak's direction. He too was motionless, but he hadn't taken his eyes off Tambov. What had long been suspected had finally been confirmed.

Tambov saw the pain and shock on Maureen's face and he leant forwards once more, reaching out a hand towards her. "Maureen, your father was a man you can be very proud of. He accepted that he had to play a terrible role for the sake of his country. He made the ultimate sacrifice. Never stop loving him. Never."

Finally, words returned to Maureen's lips. "My father helped to organise the murder of the president. He was a traitor and a criminal." She found a more fitting word forming on the tip of her tongue. "A Judas."

Tambov recoiled, tutting at her. "There are some who believe that Judas himself was not a traitor."

"Oh, so now you're a communist who's an expert on scripture? Give me a break," muttered Novak under his breath.

"I read everything that can teach me something," snapped Tambov.

"What information was in the documents you stole?" asked Maureen, her mind beginning to return to its logical, investigative state.

"They were mainly medical records. Not as dramatic as you might think."

"Then why did you tell my father about them?"

For the first time, Tambov became evasive, shifting

uncomfortably in his chair. "Maureen, I'm sorry, but that is as much as I can say. I am not American and this is an American issue. I am enjoying my retirement, away from the secrets and the lies. Please allow me to play chess in the park and admire the Lavra bell tower. This is nothing to do with me anymore."

Now it was Novak's turn to be incensed and he raised his voice. "You drop one bombshell after another and then you just decide to stop when you feel like it? When you're involved in something like this, you don't get to decide to put it behind you…"

Maureen put a hand on his arm and his voice trailed off. She turned to face Tambov and looked him directly in the eye. There was one last thread that she knew she could pull.

"Mr Tambov, I appreciate all the information that you have given us already. Please understand that I just want the truth. It is no good to me to have only half the picture. Please, if you really had the respect for my father that you claim, you will help me find out why he did what he did."

Tambov's attitude softened. "This is something you must find for yourself. And you will. Whether you like it or not, Maureen, you are your father's daughter. And he would be proud of you."

Maureen felt a lump form in her throat and she couldn't muster a reply. The two stayed staring at each other, as if a strange connection had been forged between them. It was Novak who interrupted, standing up to signal his intent to leave.

"I think it's time for us to go."

He gave Maureen a nudge and the two of them began to walk towards the front door.

"Thanks for your time, Mr Tambov. I hope you enjoy your chess and your tower," said Novak, with a hint of sarcasm.

As they entered the dim hallway Maureen stopped for a second, something that Tambov had said incidentally replaying in her mind. She doubled back and poked her head into the living room.

"One more thing."

Tambov hadn't shifted. She got the impression he was pleased she had returned. "Yes, Maureen?"

"You said that some people believe Judas wasn't a traitor?"

Tambov launched into an erratic but eloquent monologue. "Almost everyone in the world knows the story of Judas Iscariot. The man who betrayed Christ himself. A tale written into the fabric of our culture. And yet what if that was just the tale that needed to be told? There is a line of thinking that Jesus was the one who told Judas to inform the Romans of his whereabouts; that it was all part of Jesus's plan, to ensure the scriptures would be fulfilled. And yet Judas will forever be remembered as a villain. Is that not just as great a sacrifice?"

Maureen reflected on his words; it was the first time she had heard an alternative theory on such an ingrained cultural tale. She nodded and turned on her heel, leaving this strange, wild-eyed man behind.

"Maureen?" he called after her.

"Yes?"

Tambov stared at her, chewing on his lip. She sensed that he was fighting the urge to mention something else.

"You may want to look into a Dr John Cooper, I believe his name was. Another man who shares your home city," he said, his face remaining fixed in a neutral expression, before adding cryptically: "I often find that doctors have all the answers."

Maureen initially bristled with confusion before catching on to what he was referencing. "The report that you stole..."

"As I said, I don't have the answers you seek, but he might."

"Thank you."

Tambov spoke one final time. "And remember what I said about your father. Do not give up on him just yet."

CHAPTER SEVENTEEN

Later that evening, Novak left his room at the Grand Duke Hotel and walked quietly down the soft-carpeted corridor, counting the numbers on the doors until he stopped outside one that stood two down from a window that overlooked the street below. He knocked and waited patiently for a response. Nothing came. He knocked again, this time calling out Maureen's name. The door remained shut. Novak held his ear to the door and listened intently. He couldn't hear much, but there was enough to suggest that it wasn't vacant.

Novak called out once more. "Maureen! I know you're there. Please open the door."

There was a murmur inside that he couldn't understand.

"Don't think I won't kick it down. It wouldn't be my first time."

He stepped back but resisted following through on his threat. Another couple of seconds passed and then finally the sound of a lock was heard and the door was pulled open from within. The next thing Novak saw was Maureen's face, only far redder than her usual pleasant, pale complexion, with the make-up around her eyes smudged and tears still staining her eyelids. He was thrown by her appearance and found himself unsure of what to say.

She beat him to it. "Go away. I don't want to speak to you right now."

"What's the matter?" he said, to no reaction. "Can I come in?"

She looked at him coldly for a moment, with a stare that he recognised from their early meetings, eyes unblinking. However, she let her hand slip down and away from the doorframe and retreated back into her room, leaving the entrance clear for him to follow her inside.

Novak saw the room was a mess, with her belongings strewn on and around the bed. He noticed a small bottle of wine from the minibar lay empty on the floor. Maureen looked unapologetically at him, as if daring him to make a comment.

He resisted and opted for a gentler approach. "Are you all right?"

Maureen scoffed and waved a dismissive hand in his direction, before embarking on an aimless march around the room. "Am I all right?! 'Am I all right?' he asks. Oh, let's see. Not only do I now know for sure that my father was indeed behind one of the most infamous murders in American history, but that he shared his country's secrets with the enemy during a war that indirectly led to thousands of other deaths as well. A man I have spent my whole life trying to live up to, whose legacy I have wanted to emulate, is in fact one of the greatest traitors of the twentieth century."

Novak attempted to console her, approaching her cautiously. "Maureen..."

She slapped his hand away. "I bet you're delighted, aren't you? It's all worked out for you. You finally solved your investigation. Finally know the truth about the case that's haunted you. You've got everything you wanted."

Novak stayed calm, keeping his tone neutral. "No, I haven't."

She stopped wandering and stood still for a moment, looking back at him, before eventually perching on the end of the bed.

"What do you mean?"

Now it was Novak's turn to pace. "It doesn't add up. There's still something missing. I'm absolutely certain that this is not as simple as your father deciding he wanted to kill JFK, calling up his old communist buddy, and then getting Oswald to be the fall guy for him."

"Well, Tambov made it pretty clear..." said Maureen, picking at her fingertips.

"No he didn't. He became conveniently quiet when we asked about the documents he stole, the ones he showed to your father at the Presidential Library. Besides, the Soviets didn't want Kennedy dead! Everyone knows that. No, there is someone else in the background here, pulling the strings."

This perked Maureen up at last. "Perhaps that doctor he mentioned knows something."

"Exactly. We have to keep going. I have this feeling that there's more to the story."

"You trust Tambov?" Maureen asked.

"We don't really have a choice, do we? If nothing else, he seemed to respect your father, so I don't see why he would lie to... his daughter," said Novak, realising as he spoke that he had just reminded Maureen of why she was so upset in the first place.

But Maureen was lost in her thoughts, her eyes glued to the carpet. After a while, she muttered, "So we need to get back to the US then."

"Yeah, it looks that way," said Novak.

Maureen let herself fall back and collapse onto the bed, facing up at the ceiling, with her arms stretched out beyond her. It was the first time Novak had seen her look so exhausted. He quietly took a seat in a tulip chair that was tucked under a desk in the corner, leaving her to a moment of peace.

After a while she spoke, directed out at the room as much as to him. "I feel like it's breaking me, this case. You see, normally, when I investigate, I'm actually invigorated by each new revelation. It energises me, sustains me. But this, this feels as if with each new piece of information we find, it's like I lose a piece of my soul."

Novak sighed deeply and joined her in staring into space. "I know exactly what that feels like."

Maureen sat back up, now watching him. It was as though they'd realised simultaneously that the long-awaited moment had finally arrived: where a secret would be shared. Novak clenched his jaw and began to explain, his words occasionally getting caught in his throat.

"You see, I know what it feels like to lose your family. To keep them alive only in your memories. I lost my family in a car accident. My wife and my two children. In a moment, my whole life was taken from me."

Maureen felt tears rush to her eyes but she desperately held them back, trying to stay strong so Novak could continue without distraction. She'd had her suspicions about his past and his family but hadn't imagined anything quite as tragic as this.

"Why weren't you in the car?" she managed to ask softly.

Novak sighed and mumbled his way through another sentence. "My wife had left me a few months before that and had taken the kids with her. She went to live with another man, a man who had been her lover."

Maureen felt her heart sink. "Was he the one driving the car?"

This time, Novak could only nod. He looked as if all the life had been drained from his face and a blank, ashen expression overcame him. Suddenly, he seemed like a zombie, an empty, hollow image of a man.

The first tear fell down Maureen's cheek. "Novak, I'm so sorry."

He took a couple of deep breaths, willing some energy back into his body. "It's all right. It was a long time ago."

"I know, but how did you ever move on?"

"I didn't really. I knew that I was responsible. If I had managed to keep my family together, it would never have happened. And I never found out why my wife left me. She just announced it one evening and the next day she and the children were gone. I racked my brain for a reason why. What had I done wrong? Did she just stop loving me? Did she ever love me? I think, somewhere along the line, I just lost control of my marriage... like he lost control of that car."

"You can't blame yourself," said Maureen.

"Believe me, I can. And that's because I'll never know for sure. It's a case I'll never solve. The only way I can forget about it is by throwing myself into other investigations, finding the truth for others because I will never find it for myself."

Maureen nodded with realisation. "That's why you've been so invested in my father's case."

"I guess so." Novak raised his head to meet her gaze at last. "But that's not fair on you. I don't want you to suffer like I did."

"What do you mean?"

"I'm saying, if you really feel like you just described, then we can stop. Sometimes the pursuit of the truth is not worth it. If it's too painful."

"And you'd be okay with that?" asked Maureen.

"Yes. I think it should be your call."

Neither of them spoke for a while. Maureen sat silently, letting her mind assimilate the conversation. She felt tiredness creeping into every part of her, stretching down her limbs and settling in lumps above her eyes. Novak waited patiently for her answer, his hands resting in his lap, blinking away memories of his family.

When Maureen did speak, it came out as a whisper. "Perhaps we should take a break."

"A break?" asked Novak.

"Yes. Just for a while. To let the craziness stop back home. To get the people following us to leave us alone. And then in a few weeks, months, whatever, we meet again and decide whether we want to see it through. I feel like neither of us is in the right place to do that right now."

Novak thought for a while, then tucked his lower lip into his mouth and nodded solemnly.

"Okay, you're probably right."

"So shall we fly back tomorrow?" asked Maureen.

"Yeah, but it's probably too risky to fly straight back into Boston. We'll need to land somewhere else."

"Okay, that's fine with me."

Once more, neither of them was sure what to say next. It was as if, at the moment they decided to pause the investigation, there was suddenly nothing to bind them together. And as they stared at each other in the cluttered chaos of Maureen's hotel room, through tear-stained and weary eyes, there was a lingering uncertainty of what remained between them.

Maureen broke the silence. "I should probably get some sleep. It's been a long couple of days."

Novak instantly got to his feet. "Of course. I'll leave you alone."

She walked with him to the door, unlocked and opened it. He brushed past her and stepped back out into the corridor, but then turned to look at her. Maureen kept her fingers on the doorframe and met his glance.

"Goodnight, Maureen."

"Goodnight... Robert."

CHAPTER EIGHTEEN

Their flight was due to land in Philadelphia, having changed in Lisbon, all in an attempt to make their trip back to the States less obvious and hopefully harder to track. Neither of them spoke much on the flight; they had done their talking the night before. Instead, they sat in quiet, reflective moods, their respective minds on the case they had just agreed to postpone, or even stop indefinitely.

Maureen had the window seat and rested her head slackly on the adjacent panel so her eyes could see out of the slit-like pane and watch the journey unfold beneath her. As they descended enough for the clouds to part and the jagged edges of green and mossy brown landscape came into view, Maureen pondered how peaceful and organised the world seemed from above. Flying had always given her this nihilistic sensation, the sense that none of the problems of the human population amounted to much when viewed from such a lofty viewpoint.

It was also during her mid-flight musings that she realised she was landing back in the United States a different person than when she had left. Peeling back the layers of the investigation had gradually chipped away at the image she had tried to maintain of her father. Now she had met Tambov and found out about her father's involvement, not just in the assassination itself, but with the enemy she had been conditioned her entire life to hate, it was as if someone had taken a sledgehammer and smashed the portrait to pieces.

As they were walking through the arrivals gate, keeping pace with each other but with a gap big enough for a third person to fit between them, a different thought occurred to her. Glancing at Novak, she could see in his eyes that he was thinking the same. They weren't sure when they would see one another again. Neither came close to voicing the thought, but it created an uncertain atmosphere that followed them out into the terminal. As they worked their way around the barriers, Maureen looked at the faces of the people gathered to greet their families and friends. Some had signs, others flowers, but all had that same welcoming smile, coiled up and ready to spring on first noticing the face of the loved one they were waiting for. It caused a brief moment of sadness to wash over her, which she quickly pushed away.

"Right then," said Novak, clearing his throat awkwardly. "What's your plan from here?"

"I think I can get a bus that will take me to Boston," said Maureen. "It will be a long trip, but it's the best option I have."

"Yeah, good idea. I think I'll catch a taxi to the station and get the train back to New York."

Maureen nodded but wasn't sure what to say in response, so they stood in silence, facing each other at an angle, prepared to leave.

"Coffee before you head off?" suggested Novak, pointing in the direction of a small stand a few yards away from them.

"Sure," said Maureen, and they trudged slowly to join the queue.

Just then, another man appeared immediately behind them. It felt a little strange, as if he'd been racing them for the best position in line, which caused Novak to fix him with a wide-eyed stare over his shoulder, though Maureen stayed none the wiser. The man kept his head down, his face hidden by a baseball cap.

"Well, I guess this is goodbye," said Maureen, with a deliberate chuckle.

"Yes, I suppose it is," said Novak. "I think, after a bit of a rocky start, we turned out to be quite a good team in the end."

"I suppose so."

Novak seemed to wince at that, as if he'd been expecting a more definitive answer. Maureen sensed he was battling with himself, trying to both contain and expel his words at the same time.

There was now only one person in the line ahead of them. This seemed to act as a kind of trigger for Novak, who started to speak in a more forthright tone.

"Maureen..."

At that moment, a hand landed on Maureen's shoulder, making her jump. She turned to see it was the man who had joined them in the queue. Novak instinctively sidestepped to place his body between them, but two more men appeared either side of him and stopped him. It was a matter of seconds before Maureen and Novak were completely surrounded. The men were standing so close, Maureen and Novak didn't even have the space to turn around.

"What the hell?" said Maureen, feeling the panic and dread of an animal caught in a trap.

A tall, muscular man in a brown overcoat spoke to them in a deep, booming voice.

"Miss Maureen Finn. Robert Novak. I'm placing you under arrest."

Maureen's hands were roughly pulled behind her back and clipped into metal cuffs, the cold of the rims catching on the skin of her wrists. She watched as they did the same to Novak, who stood motionless, his face blank and unflinching, submissively accepting the situation. Two men now had a strong grip of their restricted arms. The tall man continued to read them their rights but Maureen wasn't listening. They had no option but to go wherever they were planning on taking them. Maureen looked at Novak desperately and he dropped his chin meekly.

"Let's go, boys," said the man, and marched assuredly ahead.

Maureen and Novak were made to follow. Their arrest certainly gained some attention in the busy terminal and Maureen felt a number of eyes on her. It was the look of a little girl, pointing at her from a distance, clearly asking her mother what was going on, that hit her the hardest. Maureen dropped her head to stare at the floor, feeling a deep sense of shame.

They felt the fresh air hit them as the automatic doors opened. There were two cars parked immediately outside, with a large, intimidating riot van behind. Novak was pushed towards the front car and Maureen watched as he was ushered into the back, the agents directing his head under the roof, as she had seen countless times on television programmes. She was only afforded a fleeting glance at him before the door to the second car was opened and she herself was shoved inside. She found it awkward to reposition herself with her hands still bound. One of the agents sat next to her, pulling her seat belt across for her and clipping it in place.

"You just sit tight, sweetheart," he said with a smug grin that made Maureen feel a burning sense of contempt towards him. She made sure she stared out of the window for the rest of the journey, ignoring the agents who were escorting her. Partly so she could better focus her mind, partly so they wouldn't see the visible concern on her face. She forced herself to take deep breaths, exhaling quietly onto the window, so that a small patch of steam periodically appeared then disappeared.

Her mind was spinning out of control, with endless possibilities occurring to her. Was she going to go to prison? Was this the end of her career as a journalist? How would her mother react? She bit into her bottom lip as a reminder to not let herself become overwhelmed. There was no way that these agents knew everything about their investigation. She just needed to wait and find out what they did know before worrying about what would happen next.

Another question popped into her mind and she found it much harder to ignore. Given what she already knew about the case, how far were the people involved prepared to go to keep the truth hidden?

The scenery outside the car told her that they were leaving the city behind and heading to the outskirts of Philadelphia. The traffic thinned and fewer cars lined the freeways they were driving on. When around half an hour had passed, Maureen noticed the car in front make a turn. Once her car had followed suit, she noticed an industrial park come into view, with large office buildings and looming warehouses. It was an empty area, with only the occasional passer-by and no more than five parked cars. They slowed and made their way into one of the parking lots outside a building with boarded-up windows. Maureen looked around for any kind of logo on its exterior, hoping to at least find out who would be interrogating them, but she could see nothing of the sort.

She watched as Novak was roughly escorted out of the car in front. He turned his face to look back towards her vehicle, but it was so abrupt that she could barely make out his expression. After a minute or so, the agents got out of her car and then opened her door to guide Maureen inside the building, still leading her forwards firmly. Inside, it appeared to be an abandoned office, with tattered old carpet coming loose at the sides lining the floor and walls bearing nail marks with old bits of paper and paint that hadn't been completely removed. Maureen was marched along the corridor until they arrived at a meeting room of sorts, where she was finally uncuffed and directed inside.

There was a worn, particleboard desk waiting for her, with a vacant chair behind it. Another chair on the opposite side was also left unclaimed. The room was poorly lit by a single neon light bulb suspended from the ceiling, the kind you might find in a corner shop, but there were still thin lines of light that sneaked through the gaps in the boards on the windows. Maureen took a seat and forced herself to take a series of controlled deep breaths. Novak was nowhere to be seen; she wondered if he was in an identical room elsewhere in the complex.

The door to the room opened and the tall, athletic-looking man entered, having removed his brown overcoat and rolled the sleeves of his white shirt up so she could see the veins on his brawny forearms. He didn't sit down on the vacant chair and instead perched on the edge of the desk, clearly intending to enjoy the questioning and, Maureen suspected, to show off to his colleagues listening in from outside.

"Allow me to introduce myself, Miss Finn. My name is Rick Nelson and I have been assigned to oversee the surveillance of yourself and Mr Novak."

"You'd better have a good reason for this. Neither of us is guilty of anything."

Nelson scrunched up his face in amusement. "Oh really? How about the theft of classified documents from the home of an FBI agent? Or the obstruction of a federal investigation? Unauthorised use of your mother's credit card, even?"

"That's not a crime. She gave that to me," objected Maureen.

Nelson smirked. "That's not how we would present it in court."

Maureen sank back in her chair, appreciating the gravity of the situation but eager not to give in without a fight.

"Where's Novak?" she asked.

"Don't worry, Mr Novak is perfectly safe. He will get his chance to talk; you were just lucky enough to get to go first."

So that was their plan, Maureen thought. Split them up and interrogate them separately, hoping one would break. This only strengthened her resolve further, as she despised the idea of being the weak link.

She looked at Nelson and tensed her jaw. "Then you should probably start asking me some questions."

Nelson grinned again and began. "Now, we know that you've just got back from a lovely holiday in Kiev, of all places, which I hear is wonderful at this time of year. And that's the thing, I really do hear. Did you really think we wouldn't have agents still stationed in that part of the world? They've spent their lives hunting KGB agents. Following a feisty journalist and a washed-up private investigator wasn't exactly a challenge for them."

"It doesn't matter that you know where we've been. You weren't able to stop us finding out what we now know about my father," said Maureen defiantly.

"Miss Finn, I'm happy to pretend that you only visited Kiev for the beetroot soup. I'm trying to be reasonable here. But now you're back in the United States, I must insist that you take your investigation no further."

"And why would we agree to that?"

He rebuked her. "There is no 'we' here. Look around; it's only you."

Maureen gritted her teeth and repressed a snarl. "Fine. Why would I do that?"

Nelson casually placed his hand on the desk, opening up his palm. "Let me put it this way: you forget about the investigation and we forget about you. You weren't exactly on our radar before you got involved with Novak and I'm pretty confident in saying that you won't be a threat to us any more afterwards. It'll be like this little escapade never happened."

"And if I decide to continue?"

Now Nelson's smirk turned into a menacing frown. "Then your life will instantly become a lot more difficult."

Maureen sat forwards and smiled slyly at Nelson. "If you think your threats are going to work, Agent Nelson, then I'm afraid you may be underestimating me."

She noticed Nelson's mouth and nose twitch violently, in what was clearly a muted flash of anger. Maureen sensed that this was a man who was not used to being challenged, especially by a woman.

"And I'm afraid you may be underestimating who you're dealing with here, Miss Finn. I can assure you we've made nuisances like you disappear for a lot less."

Maureen switched into an arrogant, journalistic persona. "Oh yeah? Do you want to tell us more about that?"

Nelson's eyes flashed with concern and he blinked himself back to focusing on the matter at hand. "Perhaps you do not appreciate the severity of your position, but let me assure you, Mr Novak does," he said. "He signed a document swearing not to disclose any of the information he dealt with during his FBI days. He's looking at some serious jail time."

Though she ensured her face remained unchanged, this revelation had broken through Maureen's defences. She was suddenly reminded that it wasn't just her life that she was playing with during this interrogation, but Novak's too. Silently reprimanding herself for her brashness, Maureen responded calmly: "Novak can look after himself. He doesn't need me to make decisions on his behalf."

Nelson grinned menacingly. "You're right, Miss Finn. He can look after himself; the question is: will he? When faced with the same questions and the potential consequences, will he be able to match your admirable resilience?"

His smugness reminded Maureen that this was exactly the kind of game he wanted to play. Forcing her and Novak to work against each other. It prompted a surge of anger and defiance inside her. She decided that she'd had enough of Nelson talking as if he had the upper hand. The agent clearly couldn't resist winning an argument, no matter what he revealed in the process, and now it was time to test that to the limit. She leant forwards and began to protest passionately right in his face.

"You're not going to stop me. I'm going to find out who my father really was and then I'm going to publish everything. I'm going to bring this web of lies that you've created crashing down!"

"Publish what?" said Nelson dismissively. "You know nothing! Sure, you've picked up on a few stories here and there, but so have hundreds of other conspiracy theorists over the last thirty years. You'll just be another lost voice, screaming into the void."

Maureen sensed her opportunity. "We know about Clipper."

She waited patiently for Nelson to respond, studying the subtle movements of his face. His face scrunched up into a patronising smirk again and he burst out into some clearly feigned laughter.

"Clipper? Who? Do you think that was a stunning revelation?"

Maureen could see that she had him right where she wanted him. She put on a disconsolate look and muttered sadly. "I thought it was an FBI code name..."

Nelson continued his cruel laughter. "Maybe I've not underestimated but rather overestimated you, Miss Finn. If you can't tell the difference between Navy and Secret Service code words, then you're really going to struggle with an investigation like this!"

It was exactly what Maureen had been waiting for. She dropped her head, as if in shame, when secretly she was biting her lip to stop herself from screaming in excitement. One of the biggest questions of their investigation had just been answered. And it had been right under her nose the whole time. Now it was just a case of how she handled the rest of her conversation with Nelson.

Continuing with the defeated act, she added, "All of that, everything we've done. And... it was all for nothing."

Finally Nelson sat down in the chair, placing his arms on the desk and meeting her dropping eyes at the same level. "Yes. I'm afraid so. Now, can't you see that none of this is worth fighting for?"

Maureen could barely hear him, her mind having left the dim interrogation room to soar back to a mental recreation of her apartment. She strained to focus. If what the agent had let slip was true, then the answer lay among the amalgamation of belongings she had accumulated there. If what she was about to do was to be worth it, she had to be sure.

Maureen said finally, "If I agree to drop the investigation, you'll leave me alone?"

Nelson was visibly excited by the prospect of her acquiescence. "Essentially... yes."

"So what do you want?"

Nelson issued his demands. "You are to return all files in your possession and cease any further activity, and you will be required to sign a document saying that you were blackmailed by Novak into helping him with the investigation, clearing you of any wrongdoing."

Maureen's heart sank. "What? He didn't blackmail me!"

Nelson tutted. "Miss Finn, think. I know how smart you are, you know what's at stake here. Think about Don Cassidy, how things ended for him. When you join this world, you forfeit the right to make friends. All you can do is look after yourself."

Maureen considered his offer, her heart thumping in her chest. She knew there was only one way of getting out of this abandoned office and back to her real life, one way of continuing with the case, one way of finally finding out the whole story about her father.

"I have one condition," she said.

"Yes?"

"Novak gets no jail time. Do whatever else you want, raid his apartment, place him under further surveillance, whatever. But he spends no time behind bars. You promise me that or we don't have a deal." She stared Nelson down, refusing to blink.

"And why should I pay attention to your demands? Does it seem like you have any power here?" he replied.

"Fine. Have it your way," replied Maureen casually. "Throw down all the evidence against both of us. Try all your dirty backstreet tricks. I've got tricks too. Do you know the contacts I have in the press? The number of people in influential positions who owe me a favour? I'm sure they would jump at the chance to publish a story about the FBI illegally interrogating American citizens and then pressing unsubstantiated charges against them."

Once more, she saw Nelson's face twitch as he weighed up the impact of what she was threatening.

She added a final blow, "If you really want this investigation to go away forever, then making a deal with me is your only option."

Tension filled the room until finally Nelson murmured under his breath. "Fine, no jail time for Novak. But everything else stops immediately."

"You have my word," said Maureen. "And you'd best keep yours too."

"Right, well that's agreed then." Nelson slapped his hand on the desk, making it shudder, before rising emphatically to his feet. "We will stop our surveillance on you once you have complied with all our demands. And then you can go back to your normal life. Though I'm afraid you won't be able to see Mr Novak again."

He began making his way to the door, but couldn't resist one final comment. "This is what happens when someone tries to dig up the past. It's better left where it is, as soil in the ground, because then you can build something better upon it. That's how we move forward. All you two managed to do was briefly threaten to slow that down."

And, with that, he left. Maureen sat alone in the eerie silence of the abandoned meeting room, lost in her own thoughts, furiously trying to piece a plan together. A plan that she had to work out entirely by herself. She would need to set things in motion and find a way to get a message to Novak, but first and foremost she needed to get back to her apartment as soon as she could.

Two agents entered the room and escorted her out of the dreary, ransacked offices and back to the car. She noticed that the one Novak had been brought in was still there, and remained empty. Maureen turned her face to the window in the car and stared blankly out of it. This time, though, she was hiding not her concern but her burning anticipation. She couldn't wait to get home, knowing what was waiting for her. Right when she had been on the verge of abandoning the investigation, she had just been given her greatest clue yet.

CHAPTER NINETEEN

Maureen waited patiently for the agents to leave her apartment. She continued with her act as the broken, disconsolate victim, keeping her chin down and talking in soft, weak whimpers when they asked her questions. When the men asked her to hand over everything from the investigation, she did so willingly, giving them the file on Tambov she had stolen from Don Cassidy, the note left in Mrs Persico's diary and the tape that Novak had slipped into her bag at Maurice's Steakhouse. She thought that that seemed like a lifetime ago and yet it hadn't been more than a couple of weeks; her sense of time had been disorientated with the combination of extraordinary events in the past few days, and the jet lag from the flight.

In return for her cooperation, the agents went around her apartment and removed the bugs they had placed there. They had positioned small microphones on her bookshelf and underneath the small table she kept her phone on. Maureen watched them closely, making sure they weren't leaving anything behind. And then they gave her a nod and made their way to the door. The agent who had grinned at her while she was escorted to the abandoned offices offered a typically obnoxious parting remark.

"Goodbye." He smirked. "Try and stay out of trouble."

"Oh, I will," said Maureen emotionlessly, and then she closed the door behind them.

She stood by the door, forcing herself to stay still, just in case they returned. The adrenaline was swirling in her limbs. She could feel herself itching to look for what she wanted, but she continued to wait. Finally, when a couple of minutes elapsed with no knock of any sort, Maureen turned sharply and stared across her apartment, observing every part of it as she tried to think where to search first. The shelf of her awards. The note from Kay Graham. The Jon Bon Jovi poster. The Celtics jersey. And of course the portrait of her father, his proud, distant expression radiating back at her. She couldn't stare at that for long.

She spotted something. In one of the lower, less organised shelves of her book collection was a kind of shoebox, decorated in a floral design with a lid that, through years of wear and tear, no longer perfectly fitted on its base. Maureen strode towards it and knelt down, lifting the lid and carelessly tossing it aside. It had been gifted to her by her mother a long time ago and, like most objects that are passed from one family member to the next, she had almost entirely forgotten its existence.

Yet she knew there was something hidden inside that might hold the key to the investigation. Most of the shoebox was filled with photos, snapshots of fond family moments from the past. There were also old birthday cards and magnets and even the odd bit of wool or string that had been discarded into the box by accident at some point. Maureen manically flicked through everything, tugging at the corners of the photos until she found the one she was looking for. There were lots of her as a child, in fancy dress, or with ice cream or spaghetti around her mouth, or feeding the ducks with a sunhat on her head.

As she came closer to the bottom of the box the photos got older, and the settings and clothing changed to reflect the different decades they were from. Now there were photos of her father in his younger days, his face brighter and more handsome, his skin less worn. She slowed down her sorting of the photos, not wanting to miss anything, taking in every last detail.

And then, all of a sudden, she found it. Taking a deep breath to slow her thumping heart, Maureen carefully untangled one photo from the jumbled mess and brought it closer to her face and further into the light. She replayed Nelson's words in her head:

"If you can't tell the difference between Navy and Secret Service code words..."

Novak had been wrong. It hadn't been an "intelligence agency thing" at all; it was a Navy thing. And perched between Maureen's fingers was a photo of her father, dressed in that iconic, resplendent white uniform, with gold buttons running down his torso and a sailor cap placed neatly on his forehead. He had served in the Navy before he worked for the CIA. And whoever had sent him that note, the one that Mrs Persico had kept hidden away for years afterwards, clearly knew him from those days. More than that, they must have had a close enough relationship with her father that one handwritten note from them was enough to change the course of his entire life.

Her father wasn't the only one in the photo. There were five men in fact, all posing at what looked like a port, with ships visible in the background. Maureen took her eyes off her father's young face and studied those next to him instead. Could any of them be Clipper? She looked intently, squinting, with the photograph no more than a few inches from her eyes, at any feature she recognised. Anything that would give her the slightest idea where to go next.

The first couple of men didn't register at all. One was short and olive-skinned; the other had a long face and a pointed chin. Maureen had never seen either before. She noticed another man had his arm resting on her father's shoulder. He was taller than her father, with a stocky build, a strong jawline and plump cheeks, with strains of blond hair poking out from beneath his cap. Maureen's brain began to whir. There was something about him that was familiar. It wasn't obvious, though: she had always been good with faces and would have been able to identify him immediately had it been someone she knew well.

Maureen examined the man and then closed her eyes, straining to think where she had seen the face before. He would have been older than in the photo when she saw him, of course, so she tried to imagine his features ageing. How he would have developed over time. And then a memory came leaping into her mind, like a great whale suddenly erupting out of the surface of a calm sea.

She was transported back a few years. Walking down a street in Southie, looking into a coffee shop window that had an emerald tint. Seeing that man, the same man who had once had his arm on her father's shoulder, lean across the table and take the hands of her mother, and squeeze them affectionately in his own.

Maureen staggered and lost her balance as she knelt, slipping clumsily onto her hip. The photo nearly fell out of her grasp but she readjusted and checked it again, making sure she wasn't deceiving herself. It wasn't perfect, of course, and there were probably close to forty years between the photo being taken and the meeting with her mother, but the eyes and jawline were identical. It was the same person, she was certain. Could this man, this figure who connected her parents at two completely different junctures of their lives, be the mystery presence who seemed to be at the heart of her investigation?

The shoebox remained open and the picture stayed wedged between her fingers for a while. Maureen allowed the information to process in her mind so she could logically plan her next steps. She needed to share her discovery with Novak first, and that meant getting a message to him that would penetrate the large chasm Nelson and the FBI had forced between them. They would need to work out what the best course of action was, in regards to their investigation. And then she needed to pay another visit to her mother's house in Southie, to confront her about what she had kept hidden for so many years.

This last thought made her feel uneasy and she walked over to her kitchen. She watched the tap run for a few seconds, poured herself a glass of water. She already felt betrayed by one parent, so she wasn't sure she could handle being betrayed by the other as well. A new thought occurred to her. If she was going to pull this off, she needed to be patient. A mistake now would jeopardise everything. This needed to be a meticulous and slow process.

And so her life returned to its previous, ordinary routine. Maureen made sure she kept an incredibly low profile, barely leaving the apartment other than to pick up essentials. She phoned her colleague at the newspaper she freelanced for on occasion and arranged a meeting to discuss potential new stories that she could work on. There was the chance to return missed calls from friends that she had neglected and to respond to further book signing invitations. Throughout it all, Maureen kept the photo on her table as a constant reminder of what she was working towards.

It surprised her how quickly this new, old routine became boring. It was as if she'd had a taste of a different life, an existence dominated by danger and mystery, filled with seducing FBI agents, interrogating ex-KGB operatives and impromptu escapes to the other side of the world. Now she had developed a craving for it. Boston felt smaller to her, and her apartment became nothing more than a cell that was preventing her from pursuing her true purpose.

One Friday, nearly two weeks after her capture and negotiation with Nelson, she decided to risk an experiment. She rang a local restaurant and booked a table for lunchtime that day, deliberately for two people. When she arrived, she asked to be sat at a table that gave her a panoramic view of the restaurant, making sure she could see every table and its occupants, looking for any sign that someone was there to observe her. That Nelson had listened in on her call or had sent someone to follow her. Maureen waited and watched, but no one was sitting alone and no one took even a passing interest in her. Maureen ordered coffee and a meal, but there remained nothing out of the ordinary. The surveillance had stopped. Nelson had been true to his word.

The time had come. Maureen paid her bill and walked to the local post office. The first stage of her delayed and long-deliberated plan needed to be put in motion. The investigation, after it had nearly suffered a permanent termination, was being dramatically resurrected.

CHAPTER TWENTY

Novak sat slumped on the floor of his apartment, his head resting against the front of the couch. He remained in the uncomfortable, stooped position, unbothered by the stress on his shoulder muscles. A bottle of whiskey was in his right hand, half-empty; he'd long ceased using a glass as a middleman. He looked up at his home, without focusing on anything in particular. In truth, he could have been anywhere in the world and he wouldn't have paid any more attention.

The events of the last couple of weeks replayed over and over in his mind. The return from Kiev, the capture by Nelson and his agents, then the brutal, gleeful way Nelson had informed him that not only was their investigation over, but that Maureen had cut a deal to lay all of the blame solely at his door.

He could still picture Nelson's eyes filling with malice as he spat the words at him in that dim, abandoned room. "She gave you up! The first chance she got! Did you honestly think she cared about you?"

More images flashed in and out of view, the alcohol causing them to merge and mix with each other, like a dark, dream-like concoction of faces and words. Maureen's face in the back of the car as they arrived outside the abandoned offices, how the agents had ransacked his home, carelessly tipping furniture over to check for hidden evidence, this time in front of his face, before they had finally removed all remaining bugs. And then, out of nowhere, Maureen again, this time fixing him with the look she had given him on their last night in Kiev, her fingertips lingering on the doorframe.

This prompted him to get angry, though he wasn't sure it was with her or himself, both for torturing himself with these memories and for being lulled into trusting her in the first place. He yelled at the top of his voice and launched the whiskey bottle at the wall, just beneath the mantelpiece. It smashed immediately upon contact, and sent dozens of glass shards skidding across the floor, spreading into the corners of the room. The remains of the whiskey seeping slowly outwards, like syrup being poured over a stack of pancakes.

After he was escorted back to New York by the FBI agents, he had essentially been placed on house arrest, with Nelson assuring him that if he tried to leave the city he would wind up in jail. All the time to himself, at the mercy of his own thoughts, had made him turn to an old friend who had previously carried him through difficult times: Jack Daniel. In the first few days, Novak had enjoyed a few glasses in the evening to ensure he could get to sleep, but it didn't take long for him to wonder what he was waiting for and for the time of his first glass to creep earlier and earlier in the day.

This had been his worst day so far. Time was not healing him, only making the wounds deeper. Initially there had been optimism, the hope that Maureen had simply done what she could to get Nelson off her back, that she would find a way to contact him and resume the investigation in secret, but with every passing day that hope had dwindled and her betrayal of him began to feel all the more real.

He pushed himself up onto the couch properly and staggered

to his feet, before ambling over to the wall beneath the mantelpiece to pick up the largest piece of the former bottle, which still had three-quarters of its base intact, its black label clinging limply to the side. Inspecting it, he saw that there was still a shallow pool of whiskey inside. He began fishing out the smaller pieces of glass that had become submerged in the liquid.

As he did, his eye was caught by the photograph on the mantelpiece above. His children smiling out at him, his son's arms gently resting on his daughter's delicate little shoulders. Novak felt embarrassed just looking at them. A lump formed in his throat and he turned back to the bottle. As he clumsily tried to pick out the glass shards, his finger was caught on the jagged edges that now ran around the neck of the smashed bottle and blood seeped out with a spurt. The pain elicited no reaction other than causing him to look closer at the edges. The dangerous, sawtooth spikes stuck out at him and he rolled the base over slowly in his palm. He had created a weapon. A weapon he could use on no one except himself.

The thought was enough to scare himself out of his zombie-like trance and he hastily dropped the bottle to the floor, deciding that drinking glass-infused whiskey out of a booby-trap was a little too ludicrous even for his new, desperate persona. Instead, he allowed himself to collapse back onto the couch. The facts of the investigation that had plagued his life for the best part of thirty years echoed out to him, like songs that he knew all the words to but desperately wanted to stop singing.

There had been more to what Tambov had told them. The mention of the doctor wasn't enough; he was just passing the buck. They had confirmation that Finn had organised Kennedy's murder and had collaborated with the Soviets to do it, but that wasn't enough either. What had Tambov told him at the Presidential Library? And who was this Clipper who seemed to be perennially lurking in the shadows?

Maureen had a point in one of her quintessential outbursts,

when she said they'd uncovered more working together for a few weeks than he had managed in years. And yet her involvement had doomed him to a point of despair that he hadn't felt for some time. It wasn't just that they had been partners on the case, it was that he had confided in her. That he had trusted someone again.

His eyes drifted over to the front door. Should he go out? There was lots to offer outside: fresh air, other people, whiskey that didn't have glass in it. He was going to have to find a new routine somehow, a reason to leave the apartment and go back out into the world. The Sean Finn case had been that reason for so long that it was going to take a while for another to take its place.

His Chesterfield coat, the one that had led to his discovery of the FBI's surveillance in the first place, was hung up on the stand next to the door. That was incentive enough. He stumbled to his feet, retrieved the coat and put it on. Making sure he had his keys and wallet, he unlocked the door and left the solace of his apartment, leaving the shards of glass still covering much of the floor.

Novak had no idea where he was going and decided to act on pure instinct. The coat had been enough to get him out of the apartment, and it wouldn't take much to dictate his next course of action. One of his neighbours was checking their mailbox on the ground floor as he drunkenly swayed down the stairs. The young man gave him a fearful, judgemental look and Novak smiled madly at him in return.

Had he had any post? He wondered if it was still being monitored by the agents in charge of his surveillance, or if they had stopped it completely. Struggling with the keys in his pocket, he gradually grasped the smaller one and fitted it into the lock to open his small, square mailbox.

As it turned out, there was lots of mail inside. A lot if it was meaningless, a selection of junk about local pizza restaurants or upcoming art shows in his neighbourhood. There were bank statements and reminders of local elections. And then, among this collection of papers and plastic, of white envelopes and coloured leaflets, was a postcard.

Novak couldn't remember the last time he'd been sent a postcard. He reached further into the box and retrieved it, before holding it to the light of the lobby so that he could see clearly the place it depicted.

The image on the front was of a river, with a pleasant collection of foliage on either side, and the wispy branches of nearby trees edging into the corners of the frame. The central focus was a small, arched bridge with black iron railings that joined the two sides of the river. It was a place that Novak recognised. This was somewhere he had been before. And the writing at the top of the image confirmed it: *Charles River Esplanade, Boston.*

Novak turned the postcard over hurriedly, longing to find out who had sent him a message. There was not much writing on the other side, just a few short sentences in neat and accomplished handwriting. He read its contents intently, before letting out a loud, animated cry as the realisation came to him.

> *Dear Robert,*
>
> *It's been too long, old friend. There are things to explain and apologies to be made.*
>
> *I am free on Sunday, if you are available. Let's meet at our usual spot.*
>
> *Your friend,*
> *Oliver Harrington*

CHAPTER TWENTY-ONE

Sunday arrived. Maureen rose early and headed for the Back Bay district. She walked past the green parasols of McGettigan's pub to take the start of the path that snaked alongside the edge of the Charles River, underneath the shadows created by the longest, finger-like branches of the nearby trees. She crossed the bridge with black iron railings, looking at the ducks swimming below. And then she slowed her brisk pace, making sure she stopped at the right bench, overlooking the river's wider basin.

She felt unmistakably apprehensive. There were too many unknowns. Had Novak got the postcard? Had he understood her code? Did he even want to see her after everything that had happened? It reminded her of the first time she had arranged to meet him, at Maurice's Steakhouse. The familiar tension in her muscles, a thin, shining layer of sweat lacing her forehead.

What she was searching for was a grey plaque bearing a familiar inscription. As she approached the bench though, it turned out to be a lot easier to locate the right one. Novak sat facing her, his face fixed with a stern, blank expression, his eyes tracking her every move. Maureen's heart rate quickened. It felt strange to see him again. And just as he'd done in Maurice's, he had made sure he got there first.

"Hello," she said, cautiously approaching the bench. "You got the message from Oliver Harrington then?"

"I did," said Novak, with no change in his stern gaze, though he leant forwards slightly on the bench to reveal the inscription dedicated to a man neither of them had ever met, but who had come to play a very significant role in their lives.

"May I sit?" asked Maureen.

"Please," said Novak, shuffling along to give her space.

Now she was closer to him, Maureen could see that he didn't look well. His eyes were bloodshot, with cloudy patches of skin around his eyelids, his skin looked red and worn and his hair was longer and wilder than she had ever known it. She thought back again to the first time she had seen him, standing in the queue at her Harvard book signing. The precise nature of his appearance had been erased. And this only added to the guilt she was already feeling.

"How did you manage to get here?" she asked.

"I made arrangements," he replied coldly. "I've got an old friend in New York, Roy Clark, who knows a thing or two about getting out of tight spots, and he owed me a favour. It won't be long until Nelson figures out I've left, though, so I need to be careful."

Maureen nodded. She was deliberately not addressing the elephant in the room, as she had no idea where to start. She couldn't quite bring herself to meet his eyes and instead stared out at the river, fiddling with the fabric of her trousers distractedly.

"Robert," she started. "I'm so sorry—"

"Stop it." He cut her off. "I'm not interested in empty apologies, I want an explanation."

"Of course." She fidgeted and stopped picking at her clothing. "During my interrogation, I realised I had missed a crucial thing.

Nelson practically gave it away himself. And I knew that I had to make our defeat convincing enough so that I could continue investigating without further disturbance. And there was no way he was going to let me do that if I didn't give him something—"

"So you gave him me," Novak interrupted again, his voice flat and his jaw clenched.

"Well, not exactly. I made him promise you'd get no jail time, but there was no way he was going to let you get away with nothing," Maureen pleaded.

"Oh I see, so I should be thanking you!" said Novak sarcastically, his anger apparent for the first time.

"No! I didn't say that..." replied Maureen, losing all sense of her argument. "What would you have done in my position?"

"I would never have betrayed you!" exploded Novak, his voice echoing out across the water, before he composed himself and dropped his chin.

Maureen was stung. "I didn't betray you. I would never do that. I just needed to buy us some time."

"You could have warned me at least," muttered Novak, tucking his arms inside his large, black overcoat.

"If I had contacted you in any way, they'd have arrested both of us!"

Novak didn't respond and raised his nose dismissively, but Maureen took that as acceptance that she had finally made a valid point.

"I have no doubt that it was difficult for you."

"You have no idea."

They sat in icy silence after that, both staring outwards. Maureen's head sunk; she had expected him to be cautious with her, but the hurt he was showing made her wonder if it was possible for the two of them to continue working together.

Finally, Novak spoke again. "I thought you were done with the investigation. That's what you said in Kiev. You said you wanted to stop."

Maureen took a deep breath and explained herself. "I know. I was exhausted and I lost sight of what we were doing this for in the first place. And then, listening to Nelson's arrogance, watching him trying to put a stop to everything, reminded me. That's why we're doing this. To expose the lies of the establishment. To find out what they have hidden from us all."

"You realise the stakes are now even higher?"

"I do, but I'm determined to see this thing through to the end now... whatever the cost."

Novak looked at her with suspicion. "What did you realise during the interrogation? What could possibly have been so important?"

Maureen turned to her bag and pulled out the photo that she had found in her apartment, handing it to him carefully. He held it close to his face and studied its contents.

She talked him through it. "We were wrong. Clipper isn't an intelligence term. My father didn't know him from his CIA days, he knew him from his time in the Navy." And then she pointed to the man that she had seen many years later. "And I think this man here might have the answers we're after."

"What makes you say that?"

"I saw him a few years ago, talking with my mother... rather intimately." She almost shuddered as she uttered the last word.

"That means your mother knows a lot more than you thought."

"I know," said Maureen coldly. "I'll go and see her. And this time I'm not leaving until she tells me the truth."

Novak's disdain towards her had eased slightly, and it was clear he was evaluating this new information. After a few moments, he asked, "You could have done that without me, so why did you need to meet me here at all?"

Maureen gulped and felt her cheeks turn red. "You were the one who started this investigation all those years ago. We've been on this journey together. It didn't feel right to finish it alone."

She looked down at the ground. Novak watched her, aware he was feeling the first stirrings of forgiveness. Taking a series of deep breaths, he leant back against the bench and stretched his back. It was nice to feel the cold breeze on his face, drifting in from the water.

Maureen continued. "Listen, I understand completely if you want nothing to do with this, or with me anymore. I appreciate that you're under greater threat than me. I just thought you deserved to know, at least."

He broke out into a dry chuckle. "What more have I got to lose, Maureen? What else can the world take from me?"

Maureen nodded, troubled by his sombre confession. "So we're back in business?"

"We are. I'm going to look into the doctor that Tambov mentioned; the one who wrote the report that he stole."

"Okay, but be careful, and don't do anything that draws too much attention."

"You know I used to work for the FBI, right?" he said with a grin.

"Where will you start?"

Novak furrowed his brow, as if physically switching back into investigative mode. "I've been thinking about it. A senior doctor like that would have to have graduated from one of the top medical schools. And colleges keep records of all their alumni. Tambov said he was from Boston, right? I figure I'll start with Harvard and work my way down."

"Sounds like a good idea."

"Thanks."

Maureen didn't respond, her mind fixed on the imminent confrontation with her mother. Novak coughed awkwardly and reverted to a serious tone, tapping his hands on his knees to indicate he was ready to get to work once more.

"Okay. Well it sounds like we both have places to be."

"How can I contact you?"

"Phone the Fairmont Hotel. I've booked a room there under an alias."

"What name?"

Novak smiled, for the first time in the whole conversation, which delighted Maureen. He shuffled slightly forwards on the bench again, to reveal the grey plaque high in its centre.

"Mr Harrington," said Maureen knowingly.

"Who else?"

Maureen nodded and rose to her feet, returning the photo to her bag. She bade Novak a quick goodbye and began walking away from the bench, her mind focused on what she needed to do. As she neared the bridge, she found herself looking back. Novak had already left in the other direction. Maureen watched him march briskly into the distance.

CHAPTER TWENTY-TWO

Harvard Medical School was in a central location in the city, so Novak decided to leave the chrome Honda Accord that he had borrowed from Roy Clark parked near the esplanade, catching the bus instead. He sat in a window seat and kept his eyes down throughout the short journey, though he lifted them to briefly inspect each new passenger who came aboard. It was liberating to be working on the case again; he found an innate pleasure in putting his mind to work after days of letting it rot in despair.

The bus stopped on a wide street with smatterings of ivory buildings and Novak crossed the road to the medical school. A luscious, military green lawn stretched out for hundreds of feet, empty and untrodden. Towards the back of the grass were a series of thin-trunked trees with broccoli-like sprouts of leaves protruding outwards. All leading to a magnificent, chalk-white building that looked more fitting of an Ancient Greek temple than a place of learning in central Boston, thanks to the six enormous pillars of its front entrance, made from chequered, marble-like stone. Rows of narrowing steps led up to the doorway, made up of three identical wooden panels. Novak admired it all for a moment before striding inside.

He found an open and bright interior, with birch furnishings and sunlight swarming in from large windows. There were sloping, curved staircases that led up to multiple levels above and atop it all a glass roof that displayed the blueish hue of the sky.

Novak headed over to the reception desk and waited to be greeted by a bespectacled, bony waif of a woman, who gave a pointed raise of her eyebrows.

"Can I help you?"

"Yes, I believe you can. I'd like to look at your alumni records, please."

The woman looked sceptically at him. "I'm afraid those records are only available to current students at the school."

Novak leant forwards and propped himself up on the edge of her desk, meeting her at eye level, lowering his voice to a whisper. "Please, you don't understand. My father... he walked out on us when I was a child. I never knew him. And I'm trying to track him down after all these years. All I have to go on is that he attended this school. I just want to find him."

His words had the desired effect and he saw the receptionist's face soften. She looked around at her colleagues buzzing around her, none in earshot.

"Okay, I'll help you. Our yearbooks of graduates are over there on the shelves in the corner. If you find your father's name, I'll be able to search for him on the system."

Novak beamed back at her and thanked her profusely, before turning and walking away with a satisfied grin on his face. The shelves were filled with perfectly organised columns of pristine red books. He sighed; this was a lot of years to search through.

Deciding the most likely decade to begin with was the forties, Novak took the first book carefully off the shelf and began scanning furiously through pages and pages of names, hoping to come across a John Cooper. Two books were flicked through without success, with no mention of the name he sought, but as he scanned through the graduating class of 1943, Novak's pulse shot up. There it was. John Cooper. Harvard graduate. Doctor. Was this the man they were looking for?

Carrying the book back to the reception desk, he waited patiently for the receptionist to become free. She looked at him with pity as he approached, holding the book open on the relevant page.

"Did you find him?"

"I think so. Could you check this man, please?" he said.

She typed away on the computer to her right, a sizeable pause each time she clicked through to another page. Novak tapped his foot impatiently. The receptionist's face underwent two opposing expressions in a matter of seconds. She made a cheerful murmur and a smile started to spread across her mouth, until it was caught halfway and instead fell downwards into a concerned frown, the colour leaving her cheeks.

"What is it?" asked Novak.

"I found him..." she started uncertainly. "The man you're looking for did indeed attend the school and went on to a long career, but I'm afraid he died a few years ago."

Novak's heart sank. His best lead had just disappeared, just when he felt he could finally reach out and touch it. His disappointment was obvious, and the receptionist tried to comfort him. "I'm so sorry, sir."

"That's okay," he replied lifelessly. "I really appreciate your help."

As he turned to leave, she called after him. "If it's any consolation, it says on our records here where he's buried. And it's not far."

Novak turned back, doubting it was worth his time, but not wanting to be rude to the woman. "Yes?"

"St Magdalene's Cemetery. I don't know if that will help you find some kind of... resolution."

"Thank you," said Novak, smiling at her. "It might."

The cemetery was located in the grounds of a charming if rickety church on the outskirts of Boston. Novak drove there more in hope than expectation, and parked the Accord on the street adjacent to the church. He pushed open a creaky iron gate and walked into the cemetery, which was bursting with wildflowers and moss. It was a small plot, with no more than a hundred gravestones, which made it easier to locate the right one.

Near the back of the grounds, just in front of a row of hedges and a view that looked up and over the surrounding countryside lay one of the newer stones, with the writing still clear upon its surface.

HERE LIES
DR JOHN COOPER
1919–1989
BELOVED HUSBAND AND FATHER

Novak stood in the quaint and tranquil spot for a moment of silence, reading the stone and listening to the sounds of birds in the distance. The busy hum of the city wasn't noticeable here and he was appreciative of the peace. It was as nice a place as any to see out eternity, he mused.

The inscription first reminded him of the similar message on Oliver Harrington's bench, before a more pressing thought struck him. *Father.* Dr John Cooper may not be alive to tell his story but his children would be.

As he reflected on this, Novak's eyes drifted below the gravestone to the earth beneath, where a bouquet of flowers had been laid, still full of colour and life. He guessed they must have been put there no more than a few days previously. Inspecting them closely, he saw there was a small piece of card tied to the stems with a ribbon, and knelt to read the message.

Miss you every day, Dad.
I'm trying my best to follow in your footsteps.
Love, Marielle

Novak's brain whirred into action. He thought of Maureen and Sean Finn, of her obsession with his legacy, of attempting to live up to the idea of her father. The very reason he now found himself at this random, isolated cemetery in the suburbs of Boston. He thought of his own father and the lasting impact he had left on him and his character. And it all began to piece together. It seemed that wherever he turned in this case, there were the shadows that parents had cast over their children. Why should Marielle Cooper be any different?

Follow in your footsteps. If she meant that literally, she had clearly followed her father into medicine. She was a doctor too. Could she have stayed local? He wondered if this fresh batch of flowers on the grave was a regular occurrence, and that therefore the latest key figure in the investigation wasn't too far away from him.

Novak sprinted back to the Accord and drove quickly away from the cemetery, stopping at the first newsagent that he passed. He purchased a copy of the local yellow pages, moved to the side of the shop and ripped the book out of its plastic. Finding the list of doctors' surgeries, he frantically scanned through, tracing his finger along the lemon-coloured paper, until he found the small square that gave him the information he craved.

Dr Marielle Cooper MD
Medical Practice
172 Melody Lane

Shrewsbury, MA 01561

Novak returned to his borrowed car, sliding onto the leather driver's seat. He took a quick swig from a soda bottle that he then tossed carelessly behind him onto the back seat, and breathed out before turning the key in the ignition. He was back on the road again.

Shrewsbury was a quiet and little-known Massachusetts town, about an hour's drive from Boston. As he got closer, the big city freeways began to blend into sleepier, sloping lanes, with grey, square houses in Dutch Colonial style appearing intermittently on either side, in between lines of large, colourful trees with leaves of military green and autumnal amber. It was a pleasant but empty place, Novak thought, sneaking glances out of the window at the scenery as he drove on.

In the centre of the town he stopped outside a grocery store and asked a passer-by where he would find the Cooper practice.

"Carry on until you hit Melody Lane, then take a right. It's tucked on the corner there, opposite the laundromat."

Novak thanked the man and followed his instructions exactly. He parked up in one of the vacant bays outside the practice, a small, rectangular building with a large front window that he guessed had once been part of a storefront. The walls had been painted an oaky brown, with a blue sign hanging above that swayed gently in the wind. Novak pushed open the front door, hearing the draught excluder rub on the fabric of the carpet.

A receptionist in a sky-blue blouse greeted him. "Good morning. Do you have an appointment?"

"I'm afraid not, but I'm happy to wait."

"Wonderful. Dr Cooper's just with a patient now but I'm sure she has a space to squeeze you in. If you could fill out this form and hand it back to me. Please take a seat anywhere while you wait. It won't be too long."

"Thank you."

He chose one of the chairs furthest away from the other patients, picking up a magazine to distract himself once he had filled out the form. Novak hated waiting rooms, which brought back memories of hospitals in his past he had tried desperately to forget.

Luckily, he didn't have to wait long. An elderly woman carefully made her way down the staircase located behind the reception desk. He looked hopefully in the receptionist's direction.

She smiled back at him. "You can go up now, Mr Novak."

Novak walked up the staircase and knocked on a door with *Dr Marielle Cooper MD* engraved on the wood. He heard a voice inside and let himself in.

The doctor swung around in her chair to face him. Marielle Cooper had long, curly hair in a striking shade of auburn red and a thin, soft face with a curved button of a nose and deep, brown eyes. She wore a white lab coat over her clothes and had placed a pair of reading glasses on her head. Novak couldn't ignore the fact she was incredibly beautiful, and was consequently a little thrown in his greeting.

"Dr Cooper?"

She offered him a welcoming smile. "Yes? Mr Novak, is it? I don't believe I've seen you before; are you new to Shrewsbury?"

"I suppose I am," said Novak, still struck by her radiant appearance.

"Please sit down," she said, gesturing him to a seat opposite her. "What can I help you with?"

Novak sat and hunched forwards. "I'm afraid I don't actually need a consultation."

"Oh, right," said Dr Cooper. "You're not one of those pharmaceutical salesmen, are you?" she added with a tone of disapproval.

Novak chuckled. "No, I'm not. I know this is going to sound

strange and I can only apologise for interrupting you at your work, but I actually want to speak with you about your father."

Dr Cooper leant gradually away from him, clearly as confused as he had expected her to be. "My father? Why? Did you know him?"

"No," he replied, feeling a little hurt by her assumption of how old he must be. "I'm a private investigator looking into cases of espionage during the cold war and I've come across a breach of private medical records in the early sixties. I believe your father wrote some of the documents that were stolen."

Dr Cooper sighed, placed her fingers to her brow and then removed the glasses from the top of her head. His news seemed to immediately exhaust her. She took her time in responding.

"You were right. It does sound strange. I appreciate that you've taken time to come and visit me, but I'm afraid I'm not going to be of much help to your investigation."

Novak wasn't discouraged. "I'm sure you must remember the work your father did. Do you have any idea who his patients were at that time? I do realise I'm asking a lot."

She looked at him uncertainly. "Are you talking about President Kennedy?"

Novak was shocked. "I'm sorry?"

"I assume you're referring to the fact my father was the president's personal physician?"

Novak tried hard to hide the mixture of confusion and anticipation he was feeling. Dr Cooper had accidentally revealed a huge piece of new information; he had always assumed that the stolen records that Tambov had shared with Sean Finn had been to do with Oswald or the plans for the assassination. He had not expected them to have anything to do with Kennedy directly. He chewed the inside of his lip, before acting as if he had heard the news hundreds of times before.

"Of course, yes. Those records on the president that were stolen, do you have any idea what information they contained?"

Dr Cooper crossed her arms and changed her expression. "Look, I'm sorry but I've only just met you and I know nothing about you. How do I even know you're an investigator? You can't expect me to talk so openly about such serious matters."

"That's fair enough, Doctor. I'll tell you the truth. I am an investigator, but I'm actually looking into the assassination of President Kennedy. I have new information that suggests there is far more to his killing than everybody thinks."

This dumbfounded her, which was the desired effect. She looked distractedly around the room, clearly struggling to decide how to react.

"This is crazy... It's nothing to do with me! I'm sorry but I'm just a doctor; this is a matter for politicians and lawyers... and I don't know," she said. "I have nothing else to say. I'm very busy... so if you'll excuse me." She gestured limply towards the door.

"Please, Dr Cooper. I wouldn't have come here if I wasn't desperate. I know that you can help me."

"Why should I?" she said indignantly.

Novak sighed. "I can appreciate that you think a lot of your father and you want to protect his reputation, but there is another daughter whose entire image of her father is threatened by this investigation. You can help her find the truth and live like you have, proudly following in your parent's footsteps."

She looked at him, her brown eyes widening, unable to keep her hands still until eventually she forced them into her lap.

"I remember when it happened. When the documents were stolen. We were living in Washington at the time. My father was incredibly anxious when he heard. Kept saying that it was dangerous, if the files ended up in the wrong hands."

"Did he speak to you about his work? Even with the president?" asked Novak.

"He never referred to it directly – I assume he had to sign a million waivers swearing secrecy or whatever – but he spoke a lot about a Mr Lance. That's what he called him. If I asked him about work, he'd say, 'I went to see Mr Lance today.' And obviously, as you grow older, you start to recognise the signs that he was working for important people. We had people over for dinner occasionally who would reference it openly. It's easy to keep secrets from the outside world, but not within your own family. So, yeah I knew what he did."

Novak continued with the softer approach, sensing he was getting closer. "I think that's sweet; parents should always keep their children away from their work. Trust me, I should know. What did he say about this Mr Lance?"

"That he was a very ill man. That he'd suffered from scarlet fever as a child and that Addison's disease had weakened his immune system. And then there was his back. My father would talk often of Mr Lance's 'poor back'. That he was in pain every single day. I guess that's what kept my father so busy."

"How did your father react to the assassination?"

She flinched. "He was very upset, obviously. We all were. But it wasn't quite what you'd expect. I overheard him saying to my mother that at least the president wouldn't have to suffer anymore."

"That's not something a doctor would say."

"We are not miracle workers, Mr Novak." Her brow furrowed briefly and her voice tightened. "That's another thing my father taught me. That as much as we have a huge responsibility, we also have to accept and respect our limits. That there is always only so much we can do. I guess he understood that better than most, working with the most powerful man on earth each day."

Her eyes drifted to look out of the window, a view of the quiet, leafy street outside, her mind clearly playing memories of her deceased father. Novak didn't interrupt her, watching her calmly as he reflected on the information she had given him.

Eventually, her attention returned to the room. "Is there anything else I can help you with?"

"One last thing, Dr Cooper. If you don't mind me asking, how did your father end up becoming personal physician to the president? That seems a fairly lucrative position to be awarded."

"My father worked in the Navy in his younger days. He was very well connected. I think a mutual friend put him in touch with the White House. It was all about surrounding the president with people he could trust, I suppose."

Novak nodded, not in the least surprised by the connection. "And I'm guessing the same people told him to keep quiet after the assassination?"

Dr Cooper nodded sadly. "Yes. I'm certain he would never have told a soul about the president's condition."

Novak rose from his chair and thanked Dr Cooper for her assistance. He could see the effect recalling unpleasant memories from her past had had on her; her eyes looked tired and her shoulders slumped lower in her chair. Leaving the elegant doctor in her room, he returned to the Accord.

Placing his hands on the wheel, but not starting the car, Novak reflected on the new information he had obtained. It was fairly well known that Kennedy had health problems, but not to the extent Dr Cooper had described. And the words of her father, that at least he wouldn't have to suffer anymore, seemed so strange and outlandish. The most pressing argument of all was that if Kennedy's personal records were in the files stolen by Tambov, why would they be relevant to the Soviet Union, and why did Sean Finn want to see them when they met at the Presidential Library?

He turned the ignition key and pulled away from the quaint, small-town clinic, his thoughts now back with Maureen. His task had been completed; everything hinged on her being just as successful with her side of the bargain.

CHAPTER TWENTY-THREE

Maureen arrived on her mother's street. Unlike her previous visit, when she was able to enjoy the nostalgic sentiment of returning to her childhood home, this time her mind was focused only on what lay in store for her when she confronted her mother. She walked on the road, heading straight to the rickety, weary house on the corner of the street. As she approached the fading wooden front door she took a deep breath and then rapped her knuckles against its rough surface.

After a few seconds it was opened and her mother's face became visible in the doorway, her greying hair tied up in a bun. She was wearing a floral dress that more closely resembled a nightgown, but she still had that signature red lipstick. Her face was fixed halfway between surprise and concern.

"Maureen?" she said in a sombre, almost passive tone. "What are you doing here?"

Maureen muttered coldly, "I need to talk to you, Mom."

It was clear Jean had sensed the animosity her daughter was feeling towards her, but she nonetheless stepped back and ushered her inside.

"Of course, yes. You should have called, sweetheart. I'd have made you something."

"I'm not hungry," said Maureen, marching straight through into the kitchen, not stopping to take her shoes or coat off. Jean followed behind tentatively.

Maureen stood at one end of the kitchen table, her eyes wide and unblinking, staring at her mother. Her heart was beating so quickly that she began to feel almost breathless. Jean looked at her with evident confusion but stayed at the other end of the kitchen. Mother and daughter stood silently in their fixed positions for a while, neither sure how to start what they undoubtedly both sensed would be an incredibly difficult and pivotal conversation.

"What is it you want to talk about, Maureen?" asked Jean eventually.

Maureen chose her words carefully. "I need you to be completely honest with me. Even if it's painful for you... or for both of us. I have been learning an awful lot about who Dad really was; and about all the things you have kept from me."

Jean's face sank and started to turn white and sullen. "What are you talking about?"

"You know, Mom," snapped Maureen, resisting the urge to scream and shout and slam her hand on the table. "I know about his involvement in the assassination of John Kennedy."

Jean put her hand to her brow and winced as if struck by an instant headache. "Maureen, I told you that searching for answers would only bring you pain. Why didn't you listen to me?"

"Because I want to know the truth!" exclaimed Maureen, her voice breaking into a yell for the first time. "Have you any idea what it's like to not know your own family? To be constantly lied to, to have been sold a dream that doesn't exist?"

She could see that tears were starting to come to her mother's eyes, but Jean held them at bay, leaning on the back of a chair to steady herself.

"What is it you want to ask me?" she muttered quietly.

Maureen reached into her pocket to retrieve the photo of her father and his friends in the Navy and slid it across the table. Jean stepped forwards to look at it.

"That man to Dad's left, I saw you with him a few years ago. Holding hands in a café in Southie. Who is he?"

Jean's eyes gave her away. They immediately flashed with recognition and surprise before darting aimlessly around the room to avoid Maureen's unrelenting gaze.

"Maureen, I don't know..."

"Don't lie!" screamed Maureen, finally giving in to her anger and emotion, sending a wild mouthful of spit across the room as she did.

"I am just trying to protect you. It's all I've ever wanted to do..." said Jean, her voice starting to crack.

"Protect me? By betraying Dad? By having an affair?"

Now her face closed up and she looked disgusted, her eyes narrowing. "How dare you!" she shouted back.

"Answer the question!"

Jean once more put her hands to her face. "Maureen, stop doing this. Please." She looked and sounded desperate, a broken woman.

"Not until I hear the truth."

Jean finally collapsed into a chair and took a series of deep breaths. "I have never had an affair with him, and I can't believe you would accuse me of that."

Maureen slowly walked over and pulled out the chair next to her, at an angle so she could face her directly, her knees a few inches from her mother's side. She was relieved to hear infidelity wasn't among her parents' growing list of crimes, but she still hadn't found the answers she had come for.

"Then tell me who he is, and how you know him. This man has been the shadow behind everything I've discovered. This phantom figure in the background. I have to know."

Jean spoke slowly, staring ahead, down the length of the table. "He was your father's best friend. Best man at our wedding. Your father trusted him more than anyone else. And since your father died, he has helped to look after me... to look after us. He is a good man."

"What's his name?"

Jean closed up again and shook her head. "Everyone used to call him Clipper... but I can't tell you his real name."

Maureen sighed. What she had suspected had been confirmed. The man in the picture, the man she had seen with her mother, the man who was behind everything in their investigation, were all the same person. Clipper. And yet that wouldn't get her anywhere. She needed more.

"Why not?"

"I know you think that finding the truth will bring you fulfilment, but I promise you that it will not. You just have to trust me that some things are better left unknown."

"Like the fact my father was a traitor?" said Maureen.

"Your father made an enormous sacrifice. We both did."

"You knew what he was going to do?"

"Not at first, but I found out, and I accepted it. Even all the pain and loneliness that came with it."

"How could you have accepted what he did?" Maureen asked with disgust.

"Your father was the best husband I could have asked for. He provided for me, looked after me, made me feel safe. He was so devoted to our family. And it broke his heart that he had to leave us. But that devotion was matched by his sense of duty to his country."

Maureen was confused, and sat back in her chair. The confrontation had come to an obvious impasse, with her relentless accusations seemingly getting her nowhere.

She changed her line of questioning. "You told me last time I was here that Dad shared his work with you. That you insisted on it. Did that ever change?"

Jean nodded solemnly. "Yes, in early nineteen sixty-three. All of a sudden, he didn't want to talk when he came back from work. He used to ask my opinion about things or tell me stories about the different cases he was working on. And then he became completely distant. Lost in his own thoughts."

"Can you remember anything specific from that time?"

Now her mother finally started to cry. It wasn't emphatic, but slowly and softly tears ran down her cheeks. Her voice wavered and cracked as she spoke. "It was the night of one of President Kennedy's speeches. Sean was absolutely glued to the television, watching every word with an almost crazy fixation. And then, after the president finished, he came over to me and hugged and kissed me suddenly, before telling me how much he loved me. That he was sorry. That he wished he had a choice. I had never seen him so emotional. That's why I have never forgotten it."

Maureen felt herself choking up and fought desperately to retain her composure. Watching her mother talk so openly and emotionally about her father was tough to deal with.

"Which speech?"

"I think it was the Commencement Address at American University. The 'We are all mortal' speech."

"And what did he do then?"

"He made a phone call."

"To Clipper?"

Jean rose suddenly from her chair and wiped her eyes and cheeks to brush away the tears. The sound of the chair legs skidding on the tiled floor screeched around the room.

"I told you I can't talk about this."

Maureen's anger returned. "Why?"

"Because you are turning into your father!" Jean yelled, projecting her head forwards to bellow the words.

Maureen wasn't sure what to say and stayed motionless in the chair.

Her mother continued. "I recognise that look. That determination in your eyes. You are just like him. And it won't get you anywhere. Look at me. I have raised you on my own. Look at what I've sacrificed. And do you know why I did it? So that you wouldn't have to suffer. So that you could have a happy and normal life. And now you're doing exactly what he did. Throwing that all away for some misplaced faith in doing the right thing."

Maureen looked at her dispassionately. "I'll be happy once I know the truth."

Jean sighed in exasperation and flung her hands upwards in despair. "That's what you think."

As Maureen continued to look at her mother, her mind began to clear and she started to take in her surroundings. Being so familiar with the house, the various objects and furniture that filled it no longer even registered with her. They had always been in the same position and had become so unremarkable to her that she had almost stopped noticing them altogether. And the photo of her parents' wedding day, which hung in a portrait frame on an exposed brick wall in the kitchen, directly opposite the cupboards, was one of those objects that had become almost invisible to her.

And yet something stuck out about it now. In the black-and-white photograph Maureen's mother and father were smiling and embracing, she in a frilled white dress with a ring of flowers atop her curls and her father in a smart suit, with a line in his hair that was slicked down perfectly. But they weren't alone. Next to her mother was another woman who resembled her. It must have been her sister, who had since emigrated to Australia and whom Maureen hadn't seen in nearly twenty years. Next to her father though, just as he had been many years before, posing at a port in his shining white uniform, was the man whose face she now couldn't unsee. The man who had comforted her mother, who she had said was her father's best friend and his best man. There, smiling out at the camera once more, was Clipper.

Maureen had been so focused on the photo that she realised she hadn't spoken for some time and her mother was looking at her expectantly.

"So you're not going to tell me?" asked Maureen.

Jean's eyes looked as if they had sunk deep into her eyelids, like headlights shining ahead on a foggy night. "No, Maureen. I'm sorry."

Maureen knew that her mother wouldn't go back on her word now. She had told her everything that she could. If she wanted to find out Clipper's true identity, she needed to look elsewhere. And she was furiously scanning through potential options in her head.

"I'm going to go, Mom," she said quietly.

Once more the tears returned to Jean's face, her cheeks scrunching tightly inwards towards her nose. It took her a few moments to mutter a reply.

"I understand," she mustered at last.

Maureen couldn't look at her any longer. Partly because she knew the sight of her mother crying would only serve to upset her, and because she knew she had outlived her usefulness to the investigation. She rose from the chair, tucking it back underneath the table carefully, retrieved the photo of her father and the five other men and then walked straight past her mother, not offering her a glance or a word of goodbye.

The outside air was welcome as she willed herself back into a more composed and focused state. As she started to walk away from the house, feeling a light breeze brush over her forearms and the gap above the collar of her coat, the idea came to her. If Clipper had been at her parents' wedding, there must have been someone else who had seen him there and would know who he was.

Maureen thought about her surroundings, about the

neighbourhood she knew so well. The different residents of the crooked houses had come and gone over the years and she couldn't be sure who would have known her parents well enough. She thought of the street around the corner, the one that was home to Sullivan's convenience store. And then it clicked. As one, the building came into her mind, as well as the person attached to it.

Along from Sullivan's, in the middle of a junction that split into two narrow, corridor-like streets, was a church. St Thomas's. A Gothic, chestnut-coloured building with a turret-like tower that swelled out of the main structure, with four symmetrical bartizans at its peak, topped with sharp, coned spikes.

It was the church she had attended more than any other in her life. The church that had hosted her baptism, communion and confirmation. That she had visited every Sunday of her childhood. The church that she guessed had hosted her parents' wedding. And overseeing all of those events was the man that she knew she needed to see, the neighbourhood priest and close family friend, Father McCluskey.

Maureen found herself jogging towards the church, adrenaline surging through her. She pushed open the door, the sound of the wood thudding against the wall behind it and echoing around the nave. St Thomas's was not large, restricted by the small area it occupied between the two terraced streets either side of it. It was dark and hazy inside, with the smell of incense immediately hitting the back of Maureen's nostrils as she entered. The aisle was flanked on either side by ten rows of pews and arched stained-glass windows depicting the fourteen stations of the cross.

To the left of the altar was a formation of candles, made up of small tealights with drop-sized, flickering flames. Stooped over them was the man she was looking for, dressed in his navy cassock. Father McCluskey was the only one in the church and he had been alerted immediately by Maureen's arrival.

Maureen strode towards him, her footsteps thundering on the stone floor. The priest came to meet her at the corner of the first pew.

"Maureen? You gave me a fright!" he said jovially, before noticing the burning, almost manic look in Maureen's eyes. "What can I help you with?"

"I have a few questions to ask you, Father, if you don't mind."

She could tell that he was worried by her manic manner, but he gestured for her to sit on the nearest bench, mustering the kindest smile he could manage.

Maureen began. "Do you remember the last time we saw each other, Father?"

"Of course; it was at your prestigious book signing at Harvard!" the priest replied.

"And do you remember what I wrote inside the book I signed for you?"

This time, he wasn't as certain. "I'm not sure I could recite it word for word?"

"I can," said Maureen. "To dear Father McCluskey, who has always guided and supported me through difficult times by giving me the faith to believe in charity, dedication and honesty."

"Very kind words indeed," said McCluskey, clearly sensing that there was more to this than simply reliving their previous encounter.

"I need you to live up to those words, Father," said Maureen. "No one has been willing to give me an answer, not even my mother."

McCluskey sighed and looked down. "Your mother has been through a lot, Maureen. And she has always acted in your best interests, I can assure you of that."

Maureen dipped her hand into her pocket to bring out the photograph. It shimmered in the flickering lights of the candles. "The man next to my father was best man at his wedding. Did you officiate that day?"

McCluskey looked at the photo earnestly. "I did. It was a happy day."

"I need you to tell me the name of this man."

The priest's face dropped and he fell silent for a while, holding the photograph between his fingers and shaking his head slowly from side to side.

"Maureen, why do you want to know this?"

"It's the final piece in my investigation. If you tell me, I can finally know the truth about my father."

"You already know the truth about your father. He was a good man."

"He was a liar and a traitor!" Maureen shouted, sending a powerful echo around the church.

Father McCluskey barely flinched, looking upon her only with sympathy. "Look at what this investigation has already done to you, my child. Would it not be better to live your life in peace instead?"

Maureen gritted her teeth. "Is living in peace worth covering up the truth? I know the Church values the sanctity of confession and the secrecy it holds above all else, but at what cost, Father?"

McCluskey remained reticent for a moment, as if his mind was briefly taken elsewhere, and Maureen took the opportunity to add a further warning.

"I have come too far now. No one is going to stop me."

The priest looked at the photo once more, clearly debating internally. After a while, he looked upwards and closed his eyes for a moment, as if in prayer, then took a deep and amplified breath, his chest visibly rising and falling beneath the fabric of the cassock.

Finally, his focus returned to Maureen. "You must promise me something, Maureen. If I tell you this man's identity, then I want you to try to move on with your life. To leave this pain for your family where it belongs, in the past."

"Yes, Father," she replied eagerly.

"Promise me," he said, looking intently into her eyes.

"I promise you."

McCluskey nodded and handed back the photograph. "The man you are looking for is called George Jones. He was a captain in the Navy at the time of your parents' wedding, but I believe he has been promoted to admiral since then."

Maureen took a while to react. The name she had been craving for so long had finally been revealed. It almost didn't sound real. Clipper had become so mythicised during the investigation that he had almost ceased to be a real person, so to hear his real name seemed strange and improper somehow.

"George Jones," Maureen said, sounding it out to herself rather than asking for confirmation.

McCluskey nodded. "Yes."

Maureen's adrenaline returned and she was itching to leave the church. "Thank you, Father."

The priest stood to allow her out of the pew, but stopped her from walking straight down the aisle to the vestibule.

"Maureen, one last thing."

"Yes, Father?"

"Remember this passage from Ephesians: Get rid of all bitterness, rage and anger, brawling and slander, along with every form of malice. Be kind and compassionate to one another, forgiving each other, just as in Christ God forgave you."

Maureen nodded politely and offered a weak smile, but she didn't have time for Bible passages now.

"Thank you."

"You must find it within yourself to forgive your parents, even your father. Only then will you find true peace."

Maureen thanked him again and bade him goodbye, before walking swiftly out of St Thomas's and back into the light of the day. Her eyes adjusted and she breathed in the fresh, incense-free air. Her mind was working in overdrive now. She was marching along the Southie streets in no time at all, looking for a payphone.

CHAPTER TWENTY-FOUR

Maureen waited in a café for Novak to pick her up in his borrowed Accord. She had phoned the Fairmont Hotel and asked for Mr Harrington, and he had immediately headed for the Public Records department at City Hall to find an address for Admiral George Jones, before setting course for Southie, Maureen and the final stage of their investigation.

Even though she was within walking distance of her mother's house, Maureen decided to stay away. She was still full of resentment towards her, despite Father McCluskey's attempts to reassure her of her mother's intentions. When she allowed her thoughts to drift as she stared blankly out of the café window, she found herself wondering if things could ever be repaired between them. There had been shaky periods in their relationship before, during Maureen's rebellious teenage years, but nothing like this. The thought made her melancholic and she forced herself to stay focused on the investigation instead.

As she was finishing her third cup of coffee, a car pulled up on the edge of the sidewalk outside, with Novak at the wheel. She hurried outside and jumped into the passenger seat.

"Did you find the address?" she asked immediately.

"Yes. He's got a house in Dover."

"Dover? Wow, what the hell do they pay Navy admirals?"

"You want to head straight there?" asked Novak, his fingers not having left the steering wheel.

"We've got to. It won't be long before Nelson works out we're back on the trail. The sooner we get there, the sooner this is finally over."

Novak didn't respond, but pulled out onto the road. Maureen noticed a knowing smile briefly form on his lips, before he furrowed his brow and concentrated on driving again. Maureen was unable either to sit still or stop talking throughout the journey. The caffeine had only added to the adrenaline already in her system. Novak, for his part, entertained her frenzied attempts at conversation, albeit with slower, more methodical responses.

"So, John Cooper was Kennedy's personal doctor?"

"Yes, that's what his daughter said."

"Which means that the files Tambov stole related specifically to the president's condition."

"Exactly. And whatever was within them was clearly very important to the Soviets, and then your father's role in the assassination."

Maureen looked at the signs and lampposts that lined the side of the road, then raised an arm and fiddled with the handle above the car window. "It feels like we have all the pieces now, doesn't it? The note at the law firm, the Hauptman Case, the meeting with Tambov, the Navy connections, the doctor's report. Now we just need someone to glue everything together."

"And that's why we're going to see George Jones," said Novak wistfully. "How did things go with your mom?"

"I don't want to talk about it," replied Maureen, and Novak left it alone.

Dover was nestled on the south banks of the Charles River, around a forty-minute drive from Boston. Novak took the Massachusetts Turnpike out towards Auburndale and then followed the curve of the river down into the greener parts of the state. The scenery became more and more beautiful – and the cost of living more and more expensive, Maureen guessed – the further south they got. They passed expansive golf clubs, edges of forests marked by lines of large oak and pine trees, glimpses of reservoirs and boating spots. It had turned out to be a bright and clear day and the colours of the trees and nearby foliage looked all the more luminous against the blue canvas above them, lit up by the rays of sun.

Seeing Novak drive for the first time impressed Maureen. Like nearly everything else he did, his approach was calm and measured, with barely a flicker of effort or emotion visible. When they made it onto the clearer roads, he pressed on the accelerator and effortlessly breezed past cars on his right. Maureen had always enjoyed being in the passenger seat of fast-moving cars; it reminded her of her wilder days spent in various ex-boyfriends' Cadillacs in her youth and it gave her a satisfying prickly sensation that ran up the length of her arms. She tried hard to make sure he didn't notice.

Their arrival into the small town was signposted by their crossing of a gorgeously quaint bridge, made of slabs of grey and chalk-like stone, with two semi-circles that hovered on the water's surface, perfectly reflected below to give the impression that the bridge was supported by two bulbous wheels. A white picket fence topped the stone parapet and Maureen looked down into the sapphire sheets of the river.

It was clear that they had entered a suburban paradise. The houses were huge, opulent and sparse. Maureen and Novak shared wide-eyed glances as they passed each one, admiring long, pebbled driveways and shining white gates, with no blade of grass left uncut on a single lush, seaweed-green lawn. Novak slowed the car to a jogger's pace, with no cars in view in front or at the rear, so that they could read any relevant signs, wondering which of the magnificent houses belonged to this man named George Jones.

Their answer came as they passed an aged but immaculate Orthodox church, so white that it was almost blinding in the sunlight. Novak stuck out an excited arm, pointing furiously out of the window of his side of the car.

"That's it. That's it! Frognal Drive. This is it."

He eased the car onto a meandering drive that sloped up towards a stately, standalone house of tawny brown wooden panels interspersed with painted blue walls, with a portico out front that was fitting of an Ancient Roman bath-house. It looked like one of the patrician houses that had homed the dynasties of Europe in times gone by. A grouping of tall pines on a circular lawn in front offered privacy from the road. It was certainly the house of someone who wished to live in seclusion.

"Jesus," muttered Novak under his breath as he pressed gently on the brakes.

They got out walked beneath the portico to a wide and burnished front door, where they exchanged a final glance.

"You ready?" asked Novak.

"Of course," replied Maureen, stretching out her hand to ring the doorbell.

They waited nervously for the door to open. Maureen's pulse skyrocketed as she heard the sounds of someone approaching, slowly turning the lock. It felt as if they had reached the final gate on their journey to the heart of the conspiracy. And now they were about to meet the gatekeeper.

The grand old door creaked open and a figure appeared within. He was tall and strong in stature, but age had softened his muscular frame and his head was covered with combed, neat strands of thick grey hair. He wore a perfectly ironed navy shirt that was tucked into high-waisted slacks with a military man's precision. And when Maureen looked at his face, the jawline and prominent, plump cheeks were the final confirmation she needed. A genuinely warm smile greeted her. This was the man they had been searching for. Admiral George Jones, in the flesh.

He didn't speak but instead quietly inspected the two of them, never once breaking his composed and dignified countenance. Maureen, in turn, took her time observing him. A moment of silent perception passed on the doorstep of the giant house.

Novak was the one to break it. "Excuse me, Admiral?"

Jones spoke softly but with a deep, forthright tone. "Yes, Mr Novak?"

Novak froze and stuttered his response. "You know my name?"

"Of course," said Jones, his voice never straying in inflexion or pitch. "You are Robert Novak and you, miss, are Maureen Finn. I have known you would be visiting my home for a while now. And I'm very pleased to finally make your acquaintance."

He had an old-fashioned charm, but there was something about the way he spoke that signified a superiority; a sense that he knew he had the upper hand.

Maureen stepped in. "Then I'm sure you also know the purpose of our visit. May we come in?"

Jones's smile widened at Maureen's request. "Of course. Let's go through to my study."

They followed him inside. He walked ahead down a long, carpeted corridor. Maureen tried to ignore the grandeur of the interior, but it was difficult. The ceilings were high, with thick wooden beams that looked like they had each been made from tree trunks found deep in the rainforest. To their left was a curved and carpeted staircase that led up to an overhanging balcony facing a magnificent chandelier. To the right, they passed shelves and tables topped with vases and ornaments from distant lands. There was even a thin, spike-like cutlass, in a pristine silver sheath, mounted on the wall.

There didn't seem to be anyone else home, with no other noise or motion detectable, as Jones showed them into his greeting room of choice, an open, rectangular space that faced out, through full-length windows, onto a narrow sliver of garden, decorated with beautiful plants and bushes in the soil on either side of the grass. The walls were wood-panelled, there were bookshelves in each corner and a small log fire was flickering away timidly. Jones sat down in an armchair beside a bar cart with a decanter and a collection of crystal glasses. Maureen and Novak sat on the sofa nearer the fire and both noticed that above it, positioned in pride of place on the mantelpiece, was a framed picture of a younger Jones, smiling next to the instantly recognisable face of John F. Kennedy.

Jones didn't speak until he had opened the decanter and filled three glasses with pungent, honey-coloured whiskey. He placed two on a tray and carried it over to Maureen and Novak, placing it on the coffee table in front of them.

"I would offer you coffee, but I think you'll find the whiskey more suitable," he said, returning to his chair.

Maureen didn't touch hers, but Novak couldn't resist a sip, swirling it around in the glass beforehand. He repressed a satisfied sigh of delight as it hit the back of his throat.

Maureen knew it was time to get down to business. "We have been investigating this case for a long time. It has taken us to the other side of the world and back. And we have risked everything professionally and personally to see it through to the end. At every stage, it seems, your presence has lingered in the background. We want to know why my father was involved in the assassination of President Kennedy. And why it has been kept hidden away for all these years."

Jones thought long and hard before he replied, tapping his fingers absently on the rim of his own glass. "I appreciate you have both sacrificed a lot in your quest for answers. And I will give them to you, but this is a long and complicated tale, I warn you. Why don't you tell me where you'd like to begin?"

"Okay," said Maureen, attempting to restrain her eagerness. "Tell us about your relationship with my father."

"Your father and I met in the Navy. He was a few years

younger than me, but he rose through the ranks quickly. And he served in my unit for a number of years before he left to join the Secret Service. He was a wonderful officer. Loyal. Determined. A man of honour. And a fiercely devoted patriot, of course. We remained friends for years after."

Maureen tried a more direct question. "In nineteen sixty-three, did you contact him when he was working at the Randall Law Firm?"

For the first time, a look of surprise flashed across Jones's face. "Now, how would you happen to know that?"

"His secretary kept the note. She gave it to me."

Jones chuckled and looked up at the ceiling. "Ah, the secretary. I was always worried about her. We gave her husband a lot of money to keep her quiet, but I guess she liked Sean too much."

"What did you ask him to do in that meeting?" asked Maureen sternly.

"I briefed him on a top-secret operation. And told him that he was the only man I would trust for the job."

"Organising the assassination of the president?"

Jones answered immediately, not breaking eye contact. "Yes."

Maureen wasn't sure where to go next. There was something so unnerving about Jones's completely unflinching honesty. It was either the manner of a man so used to conflict and death that he had become completely numb to it, or of a psychopath.

Novak stepped in. "Why was Sean Finn the only man for the job?"

"Firstly, because he had contacts with the communists. The kind of contacts he could speak to, free of the shackles of the political tensions of the time."

"Tambov," said Novak.

"Yes. One of the best agents the Soviets ever had. He was the one who brought Oswald to our attention. It was a great idea. He had all the right connections, but wasn't smart enough to be a problem. He just wanted to write his name into history, and we gave him the opening."

"How?"

"By moving the pieces around in the background. Oswald got a job at a book depository in Dallas, so we organised the presidential visit there. Open-top cars. Limited security."

Maureen felt a dryness at the back of her throat. It was all so calculated and efficient. Jones didn't seem to be relishing the retelling, or feeling any guilt either. He remained as neutral as he had been since first greeting them at the door.

"And then afterwards, were you involved with what happened to Oswald as well?"

Jones sighed and nibbled at his lip. "I admit that it all got a bit messy. We told him to run, to get away as fast as he could. But of course you can't account for everything, especially the actions of circumstantial witnesses. And, as I said, he was a bit of a live wire. Anyway, in the end we had to silence him somehow."

Novak looked bemused. "But it was all so random! His attempted escape, the arrest, the botched transfer to county, Jack Ruby! No one could have planned that."

"The more random events appear to be, the better executed the plan is," replied Jones, taking a sip of his whiskey.

Maureen had been silent for a while, allowing the two men to talk, but as she looked back at the mantelpiece photo of Jones and Kennedy she knew she couldn't restrain herself any longer. Leaping to her feet, she yelled and pointed at the Admiral.

"You madman! You orchestrate the crime of the century and you sit there and shamelessly tell us about your 'plan'. You are a criminal, a murderer! And then you sit here with a photo of your victim displayed proudly on your mantel! How dare you?" Her words caught in her throat, so she repeated them, more quietly this time. "How dare you..."

"Maureen, I can assure you that I am not mad. This was not an impulsive act of malice, but an order passed down from the highest possible authority and devised in the most structured and methodical manner. And I can also assure you that it was not a crime but a necessity."

"A necessity? To kill the president?"

"Yes. John F. Kennedy had to die."

Maureen and Novak looked at each other in disbelief, Novak gradually bowing his head. Maureen stood with mouth open and arms stretched out in front of her, her indignation reaching an apoplectic level. Still, Jones remained unmoved, nursing his whiskey.

"Who gave the order?" asked Novak.

"You have to understand the political situation at that time," began Jones. "We had just barely avoided a nuclear war! Kennedy wanted to calm things down, negotiate with the Soviets. But not everyone shared his view. There were men in very senior positions who would do anything to keep fighting. Warmongers," he said, with evident scorn.

Maureen knew of this already; Kennedy's disputes with the military and intelligence agencies had been documented by journalists and historians for years after his death. "So, it really was the establishment who were behind it after all?"

"Not exactly. I mean no one should ever have underestimated the president. He was a brilliant man. Ahead of his time in so many ways. He held them back and was starting to actually gain power behind the scenes. There was just one problem."

The realisation came suddenly upon Novak, Marielle Cooper's revelations about her father's stories reverberating around his head. He muttered to himself, "He was sick."

Maureen turned in surprise. Jones nodded, finally showing a hint of compassion.

"Indeed. He wasn't going to make it to the end of his term," the Admiral said.

"And that information was stolen by Tambov," said Maureen, joining in with the realisation. "Meaning the Soviets knew this."

"Exactly, but it wasn't them he was worried about. It was those files being leaked to his opposition in Washington that was the threat."

"Why?"

"It would give them all the ammunition they needed. It would prove the president had lied about his condition, that he was too weak to lead, his judgement was compromised. He couldn't allow it to get in the way of the disarmament policy."

"But surely that didn't mean he had to be killed?" said Maureen exasperatedly.

"I know it seems extreme, but it was better that he died as a martyr than as an invalid."

"What about FDR? He was cripplingly ill and he led the country through the war!" interjected Novak passionately.

"A lot of people blamed Roosevelt's declining health for the apparent weakness he showed to Stalin at Yalta. America is a country that needs a strong figurehead. Without it, it suffers an identity crisis," said Jones, talking about his country as if it were an old friend.

"You still haven't told us who gave you the order? If it wasn't his enemies, then you're saying it was someone close to him?"

Jones fell silent. His eyes drifted over to the mantelpiece, to the picture there. His face was filled with genuine sorrow and pain, but there was also a glint of admiration as he stared at Kennedy's beaming expression. Maureen's heart sunk and a shiver ran down her entire body. The fog cleared in her mind and she finally, truly understood.

Jones began a long, heartfelt monologue. "Jack was a Navy man too, don't forget. I first met him in nineteen forty-one, when he was just a bright and ambitious young man. Not unlike your father, Maureen. Our paths continued to cross as we rose through the ranks and we got along very well. As time went on, I spent many years serving abroad as he made waves in the political world. And then, out of the blue, he invited me to the White

House in the beginning of 1963. I was taken to the Oval Office, where it was just the two of us. I vividly remember him sitting in his chair. He was totally distant, barely even noticed me coming into the room. A look of sad serenity on his face.

"I asked him what he wanted to see me for and he told me that he needed my help. That I was the only person he could trust. He began to explain all about his condition, the potential crisis if it was ever made public, and what he wanted me to do about it. I was appalled, of course, and told him I would have no part in it. And then he said to me slowly: 'This is my last act, George. I don't want to miss my cue.'"

Jones rose from his chair and walked past Maureen, reaching out to take the photo off the mantelpiece. He looked at it solemnly and then turned it in his hand, passing it, reverse side up, into Maureen's grasp.

She noticed there was a handwritten note tucked into the back of the frame which she read silently.

> *To Admiral George Jones,*
> *I have always revered you as one of the most loyal and dutiful servants of our great country. May you continue to strive for peace, even in the most difficult of times.*
> *Your friend,*
> *Jack Kennedy*

Maureen froze, reading the note again and again, before looking up at Jones. "So he told you to order his own assassination?"

"He went further than that. He told me to find him a Judas."

"A Judas?"

"Someone to handle the operation. Who would have a

genuine reason to want him dead, if the plot was ever discovered. A traitor that would complete his tragic story. Someone who was willing to give their life to the cause."

"And that's why you approached my father."

Once more, Jones gave a reluctant and sombre nod of the head. "I never got round to telling you the other reasons that Sean was the perfect candidate. He had the potential motive. He had known Kennedy personally and they had fallen out during that awful Hauptman tragedy. We could easily spin that as him defecting if we needed to, when that was never the case. Sean was horrified, of course, but the final reason that I knew he was the only man for the job is that your father would do anything for this country. He was as brave and as dutiful as Kennedy himself."

"So he accepted?"

"Not exactly. He said he wouldn't believe it unless he heard it directly from the president's mouth. It was far too risky to organise a meeting, of course, so we slipped the message into one of his public addresses. At American University..."

Maureen's mouth fell open again. "We are all mortal," she said, in realisation.

Jones looked surprised but continued his explanation. "Your father knew Kennedy well enough, he had heard him speak plenty of times. So, for the president to not speak of hopes and dreams and brighter futures, but to dwell on the subject of mortality, it was out of character. It was a hidden message. One that Sean would understand."

"So that's why he was so upset that night," Maureen said, her thoughts immediately rushing to her mother and her father's words of affirmation and of apology to her.

"Yes. That was the night he knew he had been ordered to do the unthinkable. He helped turn a dying man into a legend. That is who your father is, Maureen. A man who made the ultimate sacrifice to ensure that the president's legacy of peace and opportunity would live on."

Once more, silence reigned. Maureen felt a current of emotion rush to her face and she couldn't stop the tears falling down her cheeks. Novak stayed rooted to his seat, shaking his head in shock, unable to deal with the answers he had sought for so long. Jones left them to their thoughts and slowly returned to his seat, pouring the final remnants of his whiskey into his mouth.

After a few moments, Maureen found her voice again. "What happened to my father afterwards? Did he really join the Peace Corps?"

"He had to," said Jones. "I made sure he was transferred to Laos. It wasn't safe for him to stay in the country. If anyone had found out, it would have looked like... well, you know exactly what it would have looked like. He was devastated to leave you and Jean behind. And he made me promise to look after you both, to make sure you were always safe. I've made sure to check in with your mother from time to time. It was her who first informed me of your intention to look into your father's history."

"Was it you who told the FBI to track us?" asked Maureen.

"I only told my contacts there to keep an eye on you. I'm guessing they were already aware of Mr Novak's prior knowledge of the case and put two and two together. They're too eager, too heavy-handed, in the way they go about things. I can only apologise if they caused you any trouble, but as I'm sure you can now appreciate, this was an extremely serious and sensitive operation."

"Caused us trouble? I was nearly sent to jail!" exclaimed Novak.

"I will see to it that you are left alone. I may be an old man but I still have friends in high places. I can assure you, Mr Novak, that you will be a free man for the rest of your days."

Novak relaxed and murmured back, bowing his head slightly, "Thank you."

"Well, what about now then?" asked Maureen. "We finally

know the truth. Are you going to stop us from telling the story? From making it public?"

Jones looked pensive for a moment, then started to smile. "No. I'm not going to stop you doing anything."

Maureen and Novak exchanged a surprised glance. "You're not?"

"Maureen, the whole point of keeping it from you was so you would grow up with a father to be proud of. Someone to inspire you as you got older. And look at all you've achieved; you can't say that it didn't work. It was only when I found out you now thought of your father as a criminal and a traitor that I could no longer hide it from you. You are his daughter. This is now your story to tell. Do with it what you will."

Maureen looked deep into the old man's eyes. He was watching her with a sympathetic, even affectionate gaze. An expression she recognised from relatives looking down to her when she was younger.

"You know, when you were born, I held you at the hospital. You fitted perfectly in my arms and weighed less than a bag of shopping. And your father was so proud that day. So happy," added Jones, before taking a deliberate breath. "He would be proud of you now as well."

Maureen choked out her response. "Thank you, Admiral."

Suddenly, Jones rose to his feet again. "Let me give you both something, as a parting gift." He walked over to one of the bookshelves in the corner of the room, returning with a leather-bound book, clipped shut at its side with a button. Placing it on the coffee table where both Novak and Maureen could see, he opened it and stretched it out so the pages within were visible.

"A collection of Kennedy's greatest speeches. One of my most treasured possessions, but now I want you to have it."

Maureen peered at the elegantly formatted words and sentences divided into sections marked with titles and dates. She closed it and held it securely to her chest.

"You'd really let us publish the story? It will cause a political crisis, a frenzy. And your own name will be tarnished."

"I told you, it is your burden now. You must decide. Though I will offer you one last piece of advice. Men like President Kennedy and Sean Finn understood one thing better than most: that the dream is the most important thing. Far bigger than their own lives and accomplishments. It is the dream that must live on."

"More important than the truth?" asked Maureen.

Jones looked at her, with a glint in his eye. "Never let the truth spoil the dream."

CHAPTER TWENTY-FIVE

They walked back to the car, neither uttering a word, the pair of them in a state of total disbelief. Novak put the key in the ignition but stared blankly out of the windscreen. Maureen gripped the edges of the book Jones had given her, running her fingers along its smooth spine. A few minutes passed, with nothing but the gentle hum of the engine. Finally, Novak broke the silence.

"So, shall we go back to Boston then?"

"Yeah," was all Maureen could manage in response.

They began their journey back to the city, once more zipping past the fringes of golf courses, the first lines of the forest and the odd glimpse of reflective patches of the river. Maureen's mind was digesting the information Jones had given them. She had finally found the truth. Now a new and equally troubling question had emerged: what was she going to do with it?

She imagined a new book, freshly printed, with a sleek, shiny front cover. Her name printed at the bottom in large, bold lettering. A list of her previous works on the inside and a picture of her next to a biography of her achievements. It would be a bestseller, she was sure of that. It might even outsell her previous book, *Truth vs State*. And yet by publishing the story that she now knew she would be disrupting one of the major events in modern American history, shattering the image that so many people held of a beloved former president.

As Novak rejoined the Turnpike at Auburndale, he spoke again:

"Where do you want to go when we're back in the city?"

Maureen had no idea. Would she just go back to her apartment and dwell on the astonishing revelations she was now burdened with, accepting her life was now going to settle in a strange, new normality? Or would she head straight to her mother, to reconcile with her as Father McCluskey had pleaded?

"I have no idea," she replied, speaking as she thought.

"I feel like I need to take a walk," said Novak.

"Yeah, good idea," said Maureen, and that seemed to be enough for him to select a destination.

He followed the roads on the outskirts of the city towards Back Bay, negotiating the increased traffic with minimal fuss. Maureen was almost jealous; focusing on the road would keep Novak's mind occupied for the time being. As the waters of the Charles River Esplanade came into view, Novak looked for a parking spot and as the car came to a stop the uncertain silence returned. He offered Maureen a weak smile and the two of them got out of the car.

They walked aimlessly along the sidewalk, looking for an entrance to the path that ran alongside the esplanade. After a few minutes they recognised the vibrant, shamrock green of the parasols that marked out McGettigan's in the distance. Maureen recalled their last visit to the pub: their argument and her subsequent storming out. A lot had changed in their relationship since then. She wasn't certain of her feelings towards Novak, and was equally terrified of thinking about the matter too deeply, but she no longer hated the stoic, smart and softly spoken man who walked beside her.

"Shall we go to the bench?" she asked him, and he nodded.

They crossed the black iron bridge that arched over a slender section of the river and continued along the path, heading for the spot that bore the dedication to Oliver Harrington. The bench was unoccupied, which was welcome, as Maureen felt it would have been inappropriate to discuss everything they had discovered in any other spot. They sat with just enough room for the familiar inscription to be visible between them, and faced out onto the water. It was a gloriously bright and pleasant day, and the light of the sun gently warmed their faces. Novak put his hands in the pockets of his overcoat and Maureen crossed her arms.

Novak began to chuckle and pointed forwards. "You see those geese out there on the water? There's a decent group of them, just perching on the surface. It reminds me of this book that I read as a boy: *The Wonderful Adventures of Nils Holgersson.*"

"I know it," said Maureen excitedly. "My parents read it to me as a child."

"I did the same with my own children," said Novak, smiling at the memory. "It's a great story. Flying away with the wild geese, into the unknown."

Maureen spoke softly. "You finally know the truth about the investigation on my father. Has that helped with... you know?"

"The loss of my family?"

"Yes," said Maureen.

"Maybe. It's certainly taught me that sometimes it's best to leave the past behind."

Maureen looked away and fidgeted awkwardly on the bench. "Is that what you think we should do? Leave this behind?"

"Honestly, I don't know. I've been thinking about it constantly. I do think Jones was right about one thing: there is no way Kennedy would occupy the place he has in our collective memory had he not died a martyr."

"So you think my father was right to do what he did?"

Novak sensed that she needed him to confirm this. "I think

what he did was incredibly brave and selfless."

Maureen nodded. "If we release the story, is that what we will be? Brave and selfless?"

Novak shrugged. "It doesn't feel like it now. I used to be sure of what the right thing to do was, but after this case I've lost sight of it somehow."

"This is the choice as I see it," stated Maureen bluntly. "Either we reveal the truth or we allow the myth to live on instead."

Novak turned his body and looked at her intently. She watched his eyes first meet hers and then drift, scanning across every detail of her face. It gave her a tingling sensation and she bit her lip in embarrassment. Then he looked down and noticed the book sticking out from the inside pocket of her coat.

"You brought the book he gave us?"

"Oh yeah," said Maureen. "I wasn't thinking, I forgot to leave it in the car." She took it out and placed it in her lap.

"Do you want to read one now?" asked Novak.

"Sure. And I know exactly which one." Maureen unclipped the clasp and opened the cover, flicking through the pages until she found what she was looking for.

At the top of the page it said:

First spoken at the Commencement Address at American University, Washington D.C. June 10th, 1963.

Maureen shifted closer to Novak, so that her arm brushed against his, and laid the book out in front of them. They read in silence, simultaneously scanning down the page before pausing at one particular paragraph.

So, let us not be blind to our differences – but let us also direct attention to our common interests and to the means by which those differences can be resolved. And if we cannot end now our differences, at least we can help make the world

*safe for diversity. For, in the final analysis, our most basic
common link is that we all inhabit this small planet. We all
breathe the same air. We all cherish our children's future. And
we are all mortal.*

Maureen closed the book and returned it to her pocket.
Novak stared out across the water, a soft smile on his lips, lost in
admiration for Kennedy's words. A thought crossed Maureen's
mind, but she couldn't bring herself to look at Novak as she asked
him the question.

"If I go and visit my mother, would you like to come with me?"

He turned in surprise, but she continued looking ahead.
"Really? You want to see her?"

"It's the right thing to do, isn't it?" she asked, clearly still
uncertain.

"It's up to you, Maureen," he replied. "All I can say is that I
know I will never see my children again, and it tears your heart to
pieces. Don't make her suffer the same punishment."

"That's settled then." As she finally stole a glance in his
direction, she noticed that he was smiling to himself.

"Do I need to bring something? It's just... been a while since I
met someone's parents," he said, and they laughed together.

Their attention was stolen for a moment by the sound of
splashing and the flapping of wings a hundred yards out in the
basin of the river as the geese took flight. One by one, they left
the water beneath them and sailed up into the sky, their great
wings beating on either side of their bodies and their feet kicking
out as if they were briefly running in the air. Maureen and Novak,
the book still open on their laps, watched their sturdy, dark
shapes continue to rise upwards, until they became distant
shadows in the light of the sun.

THE END

A NOTE FROM THE PUBLISHER

Thank you for reading this book. If you enjoyed it please do consider leaving a review on Amazon to help others find it too.

We hate typos. All of our books have been rigorously edited and proofread, but sometimes mistakes do slip through. If you have spotted a typo, please do let us know and we can get it amended within hours.

info@bloodhoundbooks.com

Printed in Great Britain
by Amazon

32863117R00133